SILENCE

by the same author

TUNES OF GLORY
HOUSEHOLD GHOSTS
THE MIND BENDERS
THE BELLS OF SHOREDITCH
SOME GORGEOUS ACCIDENT
THE COST OF LIVING LIKE THIS

SILENCE

James Kennaway

JONATHAN CAPE
THIRTY BEDFORD SQUARE

FIRST PUBLISHED 1972
© 1972 BY MARY ST JOHN HOWARD KENNAWAY

JONATHAN CAPE LTD, 30 BEDFORD SQUARE, LONDON WC1

ISBN 0 224 00689 4

PRINTED AND BOUND BY
RICHARD CLAY (THE CHAUCER PRESS) LTD, BUNGAY, SUFFOLK
PAPER MADE BY JOHN DICKINSON & CO. LTD

I would like to thank Lynn Hughes for his enthusiasm and skill in arranging for this last book of my husband's to be published. There is no more that I can say than that I feel certain James would have approved.

                      Susan Kennaway.

The doctor thought: I wish I could believe her. I wish I could take the story at its face value. I wish I could accept what the Sister had to say. I wish I could say I were a simple man, but none of us can say that any more.

He was sitting in an almost empty movie-house watching a bad western about a cowboy and an Indian girl. He thought, If I had told the hospital authorities that I too was a doctor they would have let me in, they'd have let me see Lilian, they wouldn't then have said how she was under sedation and not to be visited.

The movie wasn't very good. It had some kind of pioneering evangelist in it who didn't ring true; not, anyway, to the doctor who was himself, surprisingly, a believer. Surprisingly, because he was at the age of disbelief: over forty. But he happened to believe. He accepted the Christian rules. Which was odd, in 1968. His name was Larry Ewing, and he was one of the world's listeners.

The movie wasn't just bad; it made no sense at all. The doctor wished it would divert him. He thought, If it were half bad it would stop me thinking about their forbidding me to see my daughter. Thought, If it were a really good movie, if it were maybe *High Noon* or *Sweet Smell of Success* or even *Shane* it would also stop me thinking about the interview that lies ahead. It's years since I saw a movie. I used to go with Lilian. But now they have to put a message in. The doctor had an appointment at his son-in-law's club. His son-in-law was a fifth-generation Merchant Banker. He was very successful. He was called Mike Angel and he was a power in this club.

The doctor was funking the meeting. Otherwise he wouldn't have been sitting in an empty movie-house at 3.45 p.m. on a Sunday; he knew that. Now Lilian was the doctor's only daughter. For eighteen years out of her total twenty she had lived with him, at home, lovingly.

There is no mystery. People think of mental illness as something beyond their comprehension, to do with words like id and complex; to do with longer words than that. They listen to the drugstore analysts and feel incapable of arguing. They throw away the usual disciplines of thought. If you put someone under sedation, which only means that you help them more or less insistently to sleep, they do not then go berserk. The doctor thought, If I pass someone in the street and pretend not to recognize him it means that I do not want to speak to him. If I pass a good friend to avoid him, or even unwittingly cut him, it means, nearly always, that I am feeling guilty about him.

The doctor thought, therefore, that Lilian must herself have done something very bad; so shameful that she couldn't even confess it to him. How strange and tidy she looked, through the glass panelling: how already like a wife.

The doctor had paused beside the Sister's office, which was only a glass booth set in a carpeted corridor. It was a very expensive nursing home.

The doctor said, 'She didn't recognize me.'

He was in his tweed overcoat. He half turned away, then looked back over his shoulders. He wasn't a big man but he had a good sharp face and remarkable eyes.

The Sister said, 'It only happened last night, she's been under sedation ever since.'

The doctor never interrupted other people. He watched and waited until they had finished speaking, then either did or did not reply. In this case he did not. It takes intelligence to listen the way the doctor did.

The Sister said, 'She spoke with her husband this morning. She told him most of what had happened. You've just come at a bad moment. You're sure you won't have a little coffee? You do look rather pale.'

The doctor still watched the Sister's mouth. Then he noticed that the Sister was really quite pretty, which is the way good nurses should be. She wasn't as pretty as Lilian, but she was pretty enough for her trade. The doctor thanked her and refused the coffee. He didn't make any excuses. He just said, 'No thanks', and took the elevator.

He wished the movie amused him more. He wished he could have seen *Gunfight* or *Shane*. The moviehouse stank. The doctor buttoned up his coat and left.

Outside it was terribly cold. He thought: Maybe Lilian is really asleep lying flat on her back with her yellow hair trailing over the side of her bed; my daughter Lilian; her face a little freckled and now very pale.

* * *

'Really, Mr Angel,' the Sister had told Mike. 'If you give me your home number, I'll call you as soon as she wakes.' She referred to his wife, Lilian.

He wasn't listening to her too closely. He looked preoccupied; not quite distracted. His collar was unbuttoned and at four in the morning his chin was a shadowy blue. He was half leaning against the Sister's glass booth in the corridor and standing there, cross-legged, drinking his fifth cup of coffee, he somehow still looked rich. He wasn't a big man but he was springy and fit; almost suspiciously so, as if he felt he had a long, long way to go.

'The doses have been exceptionally strong,' the Sister said. She was quite a nice-looking, solid sort of girl.

Mike nodded. He was staring blankly at the carpet which had an infuriatingly asymmetrical pattern in yellow and orange and brown and blue.

The Sister wore the face of her watch on the inside of her wrist. As she raised it, something clicked; her cuffs were starched.

She said, 'Under such heavy sedation I'd say it would be eleven o'clock or twelve noon before we hear a peep from her.'

Then Lilian screamed. Mike moved like lightning.

'Darling, Lilian, Lilian, it's me.'

She was screaming and yelling indistinctly, 'Get away, get away.' She was more or less on her feet on the bed and stumbling back towards the wall. But the bed was on castors and it slipped a foot or two. She half fell, then, between wall and bed.

As the Sister reached across towards her she upset the low bedside light which had an expensive shade. Lilian's voice rose a pitch. Her nightie was short and white. She kept pulling it away from her body. Her blonde hair looked paradoxically tidy and orderly. Somebody must have brushed it as she went off to sleep; Mike had brushed it. Her eyes were smoky and pale blue.

'It's Mike.'

'No.'

'It's *Mike*, Lilian, darling.'

She stopped screaming. 'Oh, Michael,' she said suddenly, without emphasis or feeling. He reached out.

She took his hand, and sat down in the bed. Mike dismissed the Sister; said he'd deal with it, thank you; thank you, Sister. She went.

Lilian sat quite rigidly. She said, 'I know exactly where I am.'

'You've had a bad dream.'

'I remember everything.' Her lower lip began to tremble. Then she took in a gulp of air and steadied. She talked swiftly, almost like an English girl. There was money in her voice. She said, 'You promise not to do anything about it. Not *anything*.'

'Forget it, darling,' he reassured her. 'It never happened.'

She still sat quite rigidly. He persuaded her to lie back on the pillows. He didn't touch her shoulders or face, but kept a firm grip on her small white hand.

After a moment, she said, 'There's a difference between a girl being spoilt and not knowing it and a girl knowing she's spoilt.' Then very suddenly she sat up again and threw her arms round his neck. She said, 'Don't go away, Michael.'

'I'm right here.'

'Michael, I thought it was all over—'

'Forget it.'

'I don't mean I thought, I'll die, he'll kill me, I thought, It'll be all over with Michael, Michael won't touch me now.'

'Steady, darling, steady, don't go back.' But she had already retired too far, recalled too much. The edge of the cliff began to crumble. She didn't scream, this time, but let out a low, very frightening drone; almost a buzz.

'It's all over, my darling Lilian, don't think about it, it's over—'

But the buzz grew harder; the drone, louder. She started pulling her nightie away from her body; started to yell that she wanted a bath. 'Run a bath.' Next she was coughing, trying to make herself vomit. She withdrew from Mike again. She tore off her nightie, screaming, and lashed out with her arms and legs. She was twenty, Lilian, and her figure was perfection.

The Sister returned. She had a hypodermic syringe. Mike held his wife down and she screamed until the veins stood out in her neck.

The drug, whatever it was, worked almost instantaneously. Lilian was laid out naked, almost with that frightening, ageless calm of the dead. The nurse tucked up the bedclothes, Mike stepped out of the room. He went as far as the staircase; walked down to the landing below. He didn't want the Sister to see his red eyes or to witness his trembling like this.

He didn't smoke. He breathed deeply then he ran upstairs lightly and walked straight past the Sister's booth. He re-entered the little, single private ward. He looked at his wife's angelic face. He believed her to be the most beautiful girl on earth. He thought, Maybe she'll never be right again. Never. He didn't dare kiss her cheek lest that disturbed her. With his finger-tip he touched her hair, just where it shone, in the dim light.

Stepping back into the corridor, he gave the Sister two numbers. He wrote a note to be given to Lilian in the event of her coming round again. It was a comfortable, relaxed kind of note; composed carefully that way. He had already arranged to meet her old man for drinks at the club. In the note he casually added, ' ... and I'm not going to tell him a word about what we're both going to forget; have forgotten. Love, my darling, my forever one—Mike.'

He asked for an envelope, then he found his coat

which had a smart velvet collar. He looked, now, completely composed. As he handed over the note, he warned the Sister not to give information to anybody about Lilian. She was sure about that.

'You're very kind,' he said briefly and took the stairs, not the elevator. He ran lightly down four flights and stepped into the street. The temperature was sixteen below zero and the wind was blowing hard across the frozen lake. He set his teeth against it and half bowed his head. He had some calls to make.

* * *

On Sunday afternoons, in the wintertime, the club organized concerts. They had good people, even great people, who came and played or sang. They played Bach or sang Schubert or sent things up, like Victor Borge. The concerts were a signal, not a confirmation, of the contention that members and their wives weren't altogether philistine. And now the concert was over, the huge premises were filled with well-dressed men and women taking cocktails and telling less or more than all. Some of the past presidents—senators, bankers and railroad millionaires, portrayed within massive gilt frames themselves—looked pained by the chatter. The rooms were very high and lit only with wall lights and standard lamps with red shades. It was as if the dark area above were filled with humming-birds and rooks and the occasional wild parakeet.

The doctor had green, penetrating eyes. Even in the

crowded lobby, the porter recognized him again. As he stepped across to the bar, which was what he thought of as Angel's club, he had to take a couple of deep breaths in order to try and be calm. He told himself, don't be a fool, know yourself better, you were bound to disapprove of anyone Lilian married; but he knew too, that he didn't believe that. Thought, maybe I hate the rich. Why? Because they see nothing, that's why; because they're blind. Money protects, which is to say blunts truth.

The doctor had been there before but this afternoon he found the atmosphere unusual. It was far less noisy than the anterooms, but that was not what struck him. The difference lay in the light. The room, which was the best part of seventy feet long, had no windows. Daylight was afforded by a flat glass roof with red margins. Today the bar seemed darker because the glass was covered with two or three inches of newly fallen snow.

Michael Angel was the youngest director in the firm for which Lawrence Junior now worked. The doctor couldn't remember the name of the boy in the nursery rhyme who sold his sister for a pair of shoes, but he thought Lawrence Junior maybe sold his sister for the promise of a place on the board. But Angel, the son-in-law, was not so bad as he seemed. He looked very beautiful, brown, athletic, with bright dark eyes and very, very expensive clothes. He looked like the candidate, so to speak; the candidate for anything. But he really wasn't so bad. For instance he hadn't yet given Lawrence Junior a place on the board; which was smart of him, the doctor thought.

Now Lawrence Junior kept saying 'Literally'. He said, 'Dad, I am not talking metaphorically. No wonder Lilian's where she is. He pissed on her. Dad. Literally. Dad. Literally pissed on Lilian. Doesn't that do something to you? He pissed on her. He failed to seduce her. Failed to rape her. He drove her to this place. He drove her right there down the darkest street, just by the lake. Dad, he literally pissed on her. Or doesn't that penetrate your head?'

The doctor's son Lawrence Junior was talking with more than usual intensity, and he was often forceful and intense. He had sweat on his brow. His eyes were a little pink, maybe from the cold wind that blew outside. Junior was already fatter than the doctor. Both men needed spectacles to read the list of special Sunday cocktails in the windowless club bar. The doctor wore gold wire-rimmed spectacles: his son's were heavy, in tortoiseshell.

'She's under sedation,' the doctor said.

'You've seen her?'

'They wouldn't allow me to see her.'

'Of course they'd allow you to see her. Jesus, who's paying? You're a doctor, aren't you? Oh Dad. Why didn't you go in? Sometimes I think you like being pushed around.'

'No. I don't like being pushed around,' the doctor said, and Angel rescued him, then:

'Maybe Doc was right, Lawrence. It's good Lilian gets sleep.'

They brought the second round of Bloody Marys. Or was it the third? The boys had been there for a while, discussing things, deciding what to say to the doc.

The bar and panelling were of oak, also the few tables at the end of the room. All the fittings including the dozen or so chairs were solid and Ivy League and big. The floor was polished and red.

Because the doctor had said he did not like being pushed around Lawrence Junior waited a little before coming back into the attack. The doctor could see his game. We read our children indifferently, we do not know their hearts, but we perceive their methods, just as we recognize their lies. The doctor thought, the Bloody Marys only seem stronger because it is so cold, so very cold outside, with that wind blowing across the icy lake. The warmth of the club bar itself made him feel a little light-headed, at half past four that Sunday afternoon.

Angel said, 'Well, the long and the short of it, Doc, is that Lawrence has a plan of action and while I am not a retributive kind of man ... '

The doctor thought, Why does he use words like 'retributive'? Really, he should be a politician.

' ... far from it, I hate the idea of vendetta — but in this case I think Lawrence is right. This is an extreme case. And sooner or later a man must stand up and be called.'

Some of these phrases, the doctor thought, roll off his tongue too easily. Maybe John F. Kennedy said that about standing up and being called. Angel saw himself as a Kennedy type. His suits demonstrated that to the doctor.

Angel went on, 'In the end, we're the children of the pioneers, and even if we've gotten a little soft, we can't be that soft. We can't let somebody do that to Lilian, then just walk away.' He took a sip of the club's blood, which is what they called their Bloody Marys in Angel's club, and added, 'Or I can't. Nor can Lawrence.'

The doctor hesitated.

'Would you like some cheese, Doc? The crackers are highly recommended.'

The doctor said, 'Sister told me you were down there this morning.'

'Certainly I was.'

'She seemed a competent kind of girl. The Sister.'

'Fuck her,' Angel said, eating a couple of crackers. 'How was it with Lilian?'

'She seemed badly disturbed.'

'Right.'

'Did she make any sense to you?'

'A little,' Angel said.

'Did you find out how it happened to her?' the doctor asked.

Angel tipped back in his chair. He looked round at his friends' faces. The very blond one, Bob Dunn, said, 'Angel has a pretty good idea.'

Angel said, 'Bill, would you ask these gentlemen to stop hogging the cheese? We have a guest in the club.'

'Not for me,' the doctor said.

Angel brushed some crumbs off his lapel. The doctor screwed up his eyes.

'She was on her way back from a dance.'

'With you?'

Mike shook his head. So Hansen asked, 'What kind of dance?'

'Down at the Lakeside Youth Centre,' which was a downtown club run by uptown people.

Mike said, 'He hitched a lift with her from the club after their Saturday dance. He failed to seduce her. He hit her. He failed to rape her.' He had grown very pale. He seemed incapable of going on.

'Do you know who he is?'

'Yes I do.'

Bob Dunn said, 'Then there is something we can do, for Christ's sake. You two are not going down there on your own.' He looked round at the others, and they were with him, everyone except Walter and Tom Shaw.

Mike said, 'I'm not going anywhere. I promised Lilian that.'

'Did he hit her bad?' Dunn asked.

Mike shook his head. Then he said quickly, 'He literally pissed on her. Shoved her out of the car. Dumped her. And blew. It was about ten below zero last night, but she got to a phone. I picked her up.'

'Oh for Christ's sake,' someone else said.

The doctor said, 'Aren't the police involved?' The doctor wasn't a big man. When he asked a good question he looked a little short-sighted, looked very much like a professor who would be pushed around. Which drove his son mad.

'No, thank God. And they're not going to be. This is one of these cases when it is necessary for the husband to act privately. If you involve the police you involve the press. We don't want that.' Angel finished his Bloody Mary. One of the others persuaded the doctor to finish his drink. He was thinking, My son is very much like a guilty German; he is handsome and forceful and something hurt him, early on. Maybe he didn't like it that I never went to the army. He's right. That was one of the real reasons I studied medicine. My old man decided that. He frog-marched me to the medical school, in 1940. I felt bad because I knew it was a dodge for me, not a vocation at all. Maybe some of my guilt is visited upon this aggressive young man who is so certain that he is always right. But I haven't made too bad a doctor; my patients know that.

One of the men by the cheeseboard, in the adjoining group, said, 'Angel, it's ten of five.'

Angel nodded. He said, 'Bob, could you get them to fill a couple of flasks of this stuff?' and the doctor began to see that the plans were already laid.

He found it hard to say what was on his mind; what had been on his mind since he left the little private ward. Then he began, 'It doesn't seem that a man would go to those lengths without provocation,' and Angel cut in. He did not raise his voice but replied in the same swift smooth even tone, 'Why, isn't that a nice thing to say about your daughter? But it doesn't apply to my wife.'

There was a pause. The doctor thought, I hate him, of course.

'I don't know,' Tom Shaw joined in. 'It's never too good a thing to take the law in your own hands.'

'This isn't the law. This is private,' Dunn said. 'This is Mike's wife.'

'Right,' Mike replied. And now his suppressed anger seemed to collect itself. Bob, over by the bar, broke the awkward silence.

'Two flasks?'

'Right,' Angel said. Angel didn't carry his own cigarettes. He affected not to smoke. He grinned when he reached to a pack belonging to one of his friends. He turned back.

'So don't worry,' he told the doctor. 'I'm fortunate in my friends.'

The doctor was thinking, No wonder I went into that cinema, I must have known it was going to work out like this. The ice was clinking against the side of his glass.

He said, '*Is* it the best idea to take the law into your own hands?'

Angel said, 'He'll have his say.'

Tom Shaw added, 'That's the whole point.'

'And if he's found guilty?' the doctor asked. 'If you find him guilty?'

Nobody answered.

Somebody said, 'We don't need three cars, do we?' He was answered 'No, God no, two's enough.'

The doctor thought how strange it was that a certain type of rich man often believed that fathers had been castrated. He wondered if it was his profession, his income or merely his age that led them so brightly to this insulting assumption. He finished his vodka and very gently asked the question, 'Do I take it that we are leaving at five?'

In putting it that way, he was being less than true to himself. He was answering Angel and his friends in their own terms. He knew that. Almost as he said it he asked himself, Why on earth should I have done that? How inconsistent we are.

'Good for the Doc,' one of them said generously, thereby applauding him for having made the worst decision of his life.

Angel now mentioned a downtown address. He said, 'That is the apartment where this perverted gentleman lives.'

They were all watching the doctor as the news sank in.

'That's in the Negro quarter,' he said, at last.

'Does that alter the principle?' Angel asked. The doctor kept staring at his own shoes. 'Does it?' Angel said.

It didn't. Perfectly true. It *changed* things but it didn't alter the principle. Say nothing, doctor, if you have nothing relevant to say.

Shaw tried to help again. 'It's simply a matter of going down there and extracting the man. He'll have his say. We can hear what he says.' Somebody else agreed, 'It's as simple as that.'

Angel stood up and finished his drink. It was one

minute to five. The porter came in to tell him that the boy had brought his car to the door.

'Thank you, John,' Angel said. He led the way.

The doctor thought, I ought to go at once and call the police.

* * *

Angel's car was a Rolls, of course: the newest in navy blue. The advertisement used to say that when a Rolls was travelling a mile each minute the only sound to be heard was the ticking of the clock—and the makers were seeing to that. Heavy clods of snow thudded against the mud-guards because the city snow ploughs hadn't yet cleared the downtown lakeside highway. The temperature wasn't far below zero, but it had been cold for a week. The lake itself was frozen and the wind was still blowing across it from east of north. It threw the snow up in gusts which covered the windscreen. The lights on the dashboard shone brightly now. It was growing dark. The doctor felt cold and lonely, crouched in the back of that fast car.

Why had he said, 'Do I take it that we are leaving at five?' He liked to think it was the sight of Lilian in that little private ward which had led him into this but he knew that to be a lie. He supposed three vodkas had helped. Angel's quip had stung him, too. But in the end, he wondered, wasn't it just a vanity, a daring-do resulting from his own sense of inadequacy in that damnable atmosphere with the red linoleum, the signet rings and gold watches, the dark suits and the polished London brogues? He sat thinking these things in the car. Sat thinking, If we are true to ourselves are we ever satisfied that we are men? And if I were a simple man, I should be proud. I always used to see movies about the little men fighting back. Here I am with a son and a son-in-law both brave boys and they're not going to let anybody hurt my daughter. I should be happy. Junior must love his sister very much to do this for her.

But the doctor wasn't a simple man. He didn't behave like the plucky Jewish immigrant. He didn't really have to; not where he practised. Besides, he couldn't quite believe that the boys were reacting from love of Lilian.

Angel said, 'You know he worked at the Mission? This mission to which Lilian came twice a week? It's a friendship mission. A human rights organization. The war on poverty, right down here, somewhere. This bastard worked alongside her for quite a few weeks. Then, pow.'

'That's nothing to do with colour, Mike, not a thing like that. And you can't let it be, not whatever Lilian said, you know that.' The blond boy, Dunn, seemed to be some kind of personal assistant to Angel: he drove. Angel sat in the front beside him. In the back were Shaw, the doctor in the middle, and another younger man called Cross who was the top athlete in the group. The others followed in a big steely Buick sedan.

Apart from the clock and the thud of the snow there was soon another intermittent noise. Shaw kept talking. Shortly, the doctor began to work out why. Shaw was either more cowardly or more imaginative than the rest. He was talking compulsively. To begin with, he spoke about the weather. He went on to talk of the misery of the district into which they now penetrated. They passed from the wide freeway into a kind of temporary shanty town, then into the slums themselves.

'Right,' Dunn said, at the end of Shaw's long dissertation on the sad history of the place, and when the commentary was about to continue Angel told Cross, 'Give him a swig.' Cross had the thermos flask filled with the icy club's blood.

The doctor still kept absolutely quiet. When Shaw had swigged, he passed the flask forward to Angel who did not then forget his manners. He turned back.

'Doc?' he invited. 'It's the best Bloody Mary in the world.'

The doctor accepted the flask. He, too, took a swig then passed it forward again to his son-in-law.

Once more, Shaw began to talk. This time he seemed determined to persuade the doctor that their actions were justified. Meantime Dunn, the driver, took a drink. Angel was not a drinking man. He had sunk three or four at the club which was more than he had done for the past month. His face was a little paler than usual, his eyes brighter. He was breathing deeply as if he were trying to restrain himself.

The district maybe looked better in the snow which covered the garbage and jetsam on the sidewalks, and the bricks and bottles and old iron on the road. I'm scared of these streets, I mustn't open my mouth, the doctor thought.

Shaw began again.

'Oh, for Christ's sake,' Cross said.

Shaw said, 'I'm telling the doctor, he doesn't know it all. This bastard must have been plotting the assault the whole time ... And he'd seemed a nice young man.'

'Okay,' Angel said, trying gently to shut him up. But it isn't possible to silence a man gently when his nerve begins to go.

In the front, Dunn gave a groan. He yelled at Shaw to shut up. Angel chuckled.

About then, they slowed down. Angel and Dunn peered ahead through the snow which was blown in strange patterns by the wind. They found it hard to read the street signs. Then, passing a crossing, Dunn swore at himself. They had overshot the turning. Dunn swung the Rolls round into the middle of the avenue and turned about. Somebody hooted and swerved by in an old Mustang. He was yelling. He was black. Angel was very calm. He read out the number of the street.

Angel seemed to be changing one part of the plan, because he no longer trusted Tom Shaw. He told the driver, 'You come up with me, Bill. Tom, you stay with the car.'

Shaw at once understood the implication and began to protest. But Angel, stepping out on to the sidewalk and buttoning his black coat with the velvet collar, had authority. He did not raise his voice as he said again, 'Tom, you stay with the car.' Angel moved off towards the Buick.

Cross and the doctor had now scrambled out. They stood in the roadway, waiting for Angel. How very ugly it all is, the doctor thought. Dunn climbed out, but before he could close the door Angel turned back and restrained him, reached in and took the ignition key. Poor Shaw was too busy scrambling from the back to the front to observe this cut-off to possible flight: it isn't easy to start a Rolls without a key.

The snow helped. If it hadn't been for the snow the streets would have been crowded, but now there was nobody, except just inside the tenement door. There were some children there, staring out. Their legs looked very thin and black. One had on a navy blue anorak.

As Angel said, 'This way, gentlemen,' and led on with his gloved fingers tucked lightly into his coat pockets, the doctor wondered if he were armed. He hoped not: then glancing back and seeing coloured men emerging on to the sidewalk, he thought, I'm damned if I'll hope so.

The apartment was on the second floor, Number 217. The building was only six stories high. The snow didn't seem so thick. Perhaps the high building opposite protected the house from the wind. But some snow had drifted on to the balconies and lay against the windows and doors.

The doctor didn't know the plan of action, but it was obvious to him that everything had been worked out, beforehand. The Buick was strictly in reserve. No one had climbed out of it. The doctor thought, I shouldn't be here.

There was no need to ring or knock. The occupants of Number 217 were already on the balcony. There was an old man, a middle-aged woman, a girl about sixteen and a younger boy. Angel said, 'Good evening, Mr Clarke,' and walked straight into the apartment, with Cross on his heels. Protesting only mildly, the old man and his family followed him in. The doctor and Dunn brought up the rear.

Angel and Cross and the family moved straight into the living-room. Dunn locked the front door and then stepped into the kitchen which overlooked the balcony and also the road and the Rolls below. He switched off the lights and took up a position in which he could see outwards and downwards at an acute angle. He sat on a cheap, maybe home-made cupboard to do this.

The doctor walked through to the living-room where Angel and Cross had already started work. Like all plans, this one had already gone awry: there was no sign of the villain. Meantime Cross upturned the beds and opened every cupboard door. Pulling back a curtain he tore it off the rail.

The doctor was almost sure that there was about to be violence. It is the sins of omission, he thought, which we always live to regret. Of course I should have rung the police. Simultaneously, he observed the situation. It was fairly obvious that these were the parents and brother and sister of the boy who had assaulted Lilian. The next step would seem to be for Cross to twist the old man's arm and ask for the son's whereabouts. The Negro family stood almost in an exact line. They seemed to lack spirit. Their expressions were sorrowful rather than indignant. They did not look so frightened. It was as if they had expected the visit and in a sad sort of way were glad their time had come.

The doctor was therefore warning his son-in-law when he said, 'We can't bear the responsibility for our children all their lives. It isn't Mr Clarke's fault any more.'

But the doctor again underestimated Angel, who had style.

'What is your girl's name?' Angel asked the father.

The girl herself answered 'Christina.'

Angel didn't turn to her. He never took his eyes off the old man who was lean and creased and not very big; with a mouth that hung open.

Angel said, 'My wife, whose father, Dr Ewing, is standing there by the door, is not very much older than Christina. If I had promised to run her home, attempted and failed to seduce her, attempted and failed to rape her, then driven her to a dark place, removed her from the automobile and urinated on her, I do not imagine that you would have left the matter there.'

The mother said, 'Rex'd never done that.'

'Rex did,' Angel answered briefly.

'Not without reason, he wouldn't of,' the old man said, and Angel turned sharply away, in anger.

'Where is he?' Cross asked, woodenly.

'He's gone.'

'Gone where?' Cross asked.

'Don't say where he's going.'

Angel had recovered himself. He said, 'Why should he have disappeared if he weren't guilty?'

'Cos he know he won't get a fair shake-out, that's exactly why,' the old man said. At that point, just when the doctor was beginning to feel that things maybe weren't going to work out quite so badly as he had anticipated, there was a surge of noise outside and from the kitchen Dunn shouted, 'Angel. Here.'

Angel didn't run. The doctor followed. They looked out.

In the space of less than half a minute there was to be total bloody confusion in which men would die. Possibly, if it hadn't started in the street, Angel and Cross would have soon used violence against the family and fused an explosion, anyway; but that's not how it happened.

Ironically, the trouble stemmed from the traffic misdemeanour: the prohibited U-turn. The men in the car that had skidded to a stop were belligerent and not quite sober. Maybe their club too had blood. Whatever, they had enough liquor in them to persevere. They followed in the Buick's track: then parked behind it.

Now, joined by a dozen other Negroes who had appeared on the sidewalk, they were shouting and rocking the Buick. The noise they made brought everybody on to the street. As Angel and the doctor watched, the car was overturned, with its occupants trapped inside.

There were screams and shouts. Then a shot was fired. Shaw had found the gun that Angel always kept in the pocket of the Rolls. He fired back towards the group round the Buick: fired wildly, but winged one man. He leapt back into the car only to find that the key wasn't there. His fingers fumbled up and down the dashboard. With a little yelp of fear, he jumped out into the road again and backed away. Frightened by the growing crowd he fired several more shots, but above their heads. He then took to his heels and ran.

Dunn, Cross, Angel and the doctor were by this time out of apartment 217 and running along the balcony, but they were far, far too late. There wasn't one man, not even one dozen: every man for miles around seemed to be converging from above and below. And there were more and more running up the street. They went to the Buick, to help kick in Whitey's head, or else they joined the mob by the stone stairs.

It was to take many days before the doctor worked out just what happened next. Only one got clean away. Angel, in the Rolls. Lawrence Junior fled in the other direction. The doctor managed to throw himself across the car, over the trunk at the back but he got flung clear at the first corner. About fifty black people were pouring out of the tenement. The doctor ran blindly until he thought his legs and heart would break. He kept stumbling and falling and each place where he fell he left red marks in the snow. The blood was coming from a knife wound in his side.

* * *

The wound was in his side just above the trouser belt and he suspected that his liver was punctured, which would give him an hour or two, not more. But still he ran and staggered and fell and picked himself up again. He was, at this point, no braver than Tom Shaw or any other frightened man.

In fact he was saved by the wind and the snow. Had it been better weather there would have been people in the street. Had it been calm the drifting snow would not have covered his trail of redness.

Turning at the first crossing, in what he imagined to be an uptown direction, he saw what he had hoped for: a telephone kiosk. He kept striking the building with the side of his fist as if that helped to push him along. He thought, Steady. I dial Emergency, that's all I have to do. But then he remembered that he had no idea where he was. He ran back to the crossing to get the numbers of street and avenue, which were still a long, long way downtown. The street sign was covered with snow and the light wasn't clear. He banged the signpost so that the snow would fall away and reveal the writing. The snow fell in his face and he wiped it away with his sleeve. He was still staring up at it when a car suddenly swung into the street. Its headlights dazzled him for a moment. He turned and started to run back to the kiosk.

But he never reached it. The car too, turned at the crossing. It skidded in the loose snow. It was coming very fast. As it revved and followed the kerb behind him, he crazily hurtled straight across the street then started to run back to the crossing. The car drew up by the phone opposite. The doctor cowered into a dark doorstep beside a shop that was boarded up— Premises To Let. A couple climbed out of the car. They both went into the kiosk. For a moment the doctor couldn't believe his luck. He stood pressing his shoulder against the lintel.

The door behind him opened up. It wasn't locked.

The doctor's wound did not hurt him too badly, but he was beginning to shake. It wasn't only the pain that made him tremble. It was what he had seen back there: in the fighting one of their children, a boy about twelve, was shoved over the edge of the balcony and he must have been hurt very badly. The doctor thought, They will kill me, lynch me, tear me apart.

The couple left the kiosk and jumped into their big car. The young man started it foolishly again and his wheels spun round in the snow. Then he skidded off into the distance. The doctor moved up the street in the shadows but before he had even stepped into the light, he heard the pursuers. This time there was no mistake. There were three or four cars. One stopped at the crossing and five or six men got out. They were debating which side of the street they should take. They were searching for him. He thought, Somebody must have seen me fall off the back of the Rolls. Hark, hark the dogs do bark.

Keeping in the shadow he stepped swiftly back towards the shop with the shutters and the broken front door. Quickly he stepped inside. For some extraordinary reason, no kid had bothered to break the frosted glass in the door. The doctor thought he could hear the hunters trying the doors farther down the street. He knew he was panicking. He could see himself from above. He thought he'd better lie down on the floor with his back against the door. He did so, dropping down just as a couple more cars swung by. He could hear the men in the cars shouting, 'We'll find him. Keep a look out for the footsteps in the snow.' Then the car was gone.

The doctor crouched and held his breath. He couldn't hear anybody now. Like anyone who has let fear take its grip he was unable to act consistently any more. He almost wanted to give himself up. How like me, he thought. At the worst possible moment, at the instant of maximum risk, as he heard the men just coming up alongside, he moved and ran across the hall, up the first flight of stairs. There was a bulb burning on the landing above. The walls of the place were painted marine blue. He *must* have thrown a shadow on the frosted glass.

He heard their voices again. They seemed to have paused. They were talking about the phone kiosk. Another two cars came by and one stopped. It seemed that more men were getting out, though the doctor couldn't see. He imagined hundreds, with sticks and oily cloths round their hair. And with that he heard dogs. He thought he heard the bark of a dog. That made him stagger up the second flight of stairs. He thought, I'll hide. I'll find some cover, then get back to the phone when they've gone. In the distance there was the sound of sirens: of police cars and ambulances; of a fire engine, maybe, to wash away the red snow.

At the top of the first flight of stairs, on the mean landing facing him, there was a door which would lead into a room overlooking the street and it seemed to be open. They must have seen that the building is deserted, he thought, they must have guessed that he'd come in here. The snow and the sweat had made his face wet and when he tried to wipe his eyes clear he left blood on his cheeks. Hark, hark, he thought, the dogs do bark; he used to tell Lilian all those rhymes. God, how the mind flits and yet sticks when we finally panic. What a white skin I have, the doctor thought. How irrelevant is the mind, in fear.

The door in front of the doctor must have had some story. Again the doctor's mind switched in that haphazard, tripping, incredibly swift way: this time, to the imagined story of the door.

The voices were calling outside: and calling back.

There wasn't a lock on the door; there was, so to speak, a no-lock. The lock that had been there was battered away; amputated. Axed, axed out and replaced by plywood and boxwood all nailed together; and some kind of hook and chain. Chain to the lintel.

Another car had drawn up outside in the snowy street. Men with black voices were asking each other, 'Left, Right, this way, that?'

So somebody sometime must have broken into this room, maybe yelling to get at a woman or to set free a child or a dog, or to mend some broken pipe.

The doctor moved in, suddenly, and the chain rattled against his hand as he stepped into the dark. Inside, the doctor fumbled with the chain. He could still hear those voices out there.

If he hooked up the chain, then nobody could open the door from outside. Not if he hooked it properly and twisted and knotted it. The doctor did that, frantically; tied it, looped it, pulled it. Fear. There was no kind of padlock, but the hook seemed strong. So tie it again, the doctor told himself, you will be safe for a second or two, even for half a minute, safe from every damn black-power running dog downstairs and outside in the bleak street. Safe maybe for a minute.

As he tried it again, and the chain zipped and rattled in his nervous hands, the doctor kept saying to himself, 'Safe, safe', only 'safe'. The doctor thought, Three club drinks, that stage just before group drunkenness where you see your own complexion reflected in the ruddiness of the others' faces. He felt ashamed. Tabasco on the old liver wound. He shivered and breathed out his held breath. He thought, The window must be covered up. I must go to the window and watch the street from there: watch the kiosk; wait my time.

He breathed again, feeling his knees sag.

Then, all of a sudden his body reacted. His body reacted before his mind. His spine, his legs, his fingers even stiffened. His mouth went dry. His hair stood up at the back of his neck. Then he froze. Absolutely froze. He closed his eyes shut and hung on to the chain behind his back.

The doctor knew that he was not alone in the room.

* * *

The doctor came round again as he hit the floor. He groaned. His sense of fear awoke before his power of reason and before his pain. He suppressed his groan. He did not dare close his eyes. He stared at the darkness which must have been the floor, stared at it as if he was no longer capable of closing his eyes.

The doctor knew that he was behaving like a coward. He thought, Worse than talkative Tom Shaw. Then, at once, he tried to reason with himself. Said, 'Don't too easily condemn yourself. That never helps. There's a difference between unnecessary cowardice and justifiable fear.'

He could hear It breathing. He knew It was awake. The door was chained, tied up in knots. The room was almost totally dark. Almost. Perhaps a dog, he thought, a wild dog.

The voices were dying away. Perhaps snow was falling more heavily. They'd lost the track ... Now he was sorry they'd lost the track.

The doctor stayed absolutely still, as rigid as a stone, listening to the faint, faint sound of breathing. He was quite sure he heard the breathing. He was almost certain that he was in the presence of an animal. Then he thought, No, there are many people in here. He strained to listen as he had never listened. The breathing was regular. He must look up.

He did so, and yelped, and lay back.

He had seen absolutely nothing. But the sound of his own emasculated voice brought him a little to his senses. He was now in a different position, his back more or less against the door. He was behaving like a schoolgirl in a haunted house. He could see that. The pain—sudden, hot, wet pain—from his side helped his control. The touch of the blood greatly encouraged him. He dared lift his eyes.

The room was no longer totally dark. He could make out the rectangle of the window, which seemed to be covered with some kind of sacking or cloth. Then below that rectangle, in what seemed to be the corner of the room, there were two holes, two sources of light. For a moment the doctor thought that they must be peepholes into an adjoining room in which there was light. But something about the angles made that hard to accept. The light must therefore be reflected. Perhaps there was something metal or glass on a shelf.

The two sources moved. Again the doctor let out a little yelp of terror, then at once suppressed it. They were eyes. They were eyes and he was on the floor, his back to a door that would take a minute to open. Maybe they were dog's eyes, after all. They seemed to be yellow, but the colour was hard to tell in the street light.

Because the eyes were at a low level in the room the

doctor kept asking himself what kind of animal they might belong to. But the mind, always complex, is more than ever so, in fear. It appears to be frozen but, in truth, it is in ten places at once. Even as he went through the list from police-dog to chimpanzee, the doctor didn't believe himself. He knew he was locked in the room with another human being; and not a white one. He hardly dared recognize the odds he was really reckoning; the animal choice was only a cover to the important, more frightening calculation.

It was the door that made him think of a lunatic. It was a fugitive's door. And it had recently been broken down, axed down, maybe more than once. The room was barely heated, and apparently unfurnished. It followed that it was the resting place of some hermit, some untouchable.

Again almost imperceptively, the eyes moved. Now there was no shouting in the street any more. The doctor's shoes and trousers were soaking wet from the snow. His shirt was wet from the blood and the sweat. He felt both cold and warm at once. He thought, What a poor kind of soldier I would have made. I have acted to preserve myself. I have run. Have escaped. Have closed the door. But he could not bring himself to try more. He was aware of his self-pity as he closed his eyes again and fell half back to sleep. Faintly aware, too, that this whole mood of surrender, this opiate feeling was in truth a ruse. It was a message to the monster in the corner of the room: pity me.

At last, the eyes turned away. A long arm reached

out towards the corner of the cloth by the window and opened up a bright triangular patch of light. A long black arm, with bangles on it. The light shone like an arc on to a bed without sheets. And then this thing, this person shifted across the bed, into the light which now seemed curiously green. She unwrapped the blanket in which she had been lying.

She was very big, she was most certainly 'she', wearing diamanté buttons over her nipples, and she was decked up, more or less, like a vaudeville bride. Her hair was dyed not golden but light brown. She wore some kind of tiara in it which held up a strange veil. Perhaps she was a mad, abandoned bride, the doctor thought. She had long finger-nails covered in silver polish, except for the index finger which was a dark brown kind of colour in this light: but which the doctor rightly reckoned to be red. Round her waist she wore a velvet strap decorated, again, with diamanté. She had white, apparently luminous panties on. They were the size of the briefest bikini. After that came her enormous, powerful long thighs and calves. She had the body of an Olympic sportswoman. She wore satin slippers on her feet.

The doctor sat absolutely still. The female said nothing. She lay on the bed looking his way, dangling her slipper on her toe. There was a sound, again, from the street. The doctor knew that in the light his face must look very white. She only had to reach behind her and knock one of her bracelets or big rings against the window pane. The boys would hear it and come up and do the rest.

She reached up her arm. The doctor heard himself say, 'Please don't.'

She kept her hand up at the window.

The doctor said, 'I'm bleeding to death.'

She still kept her hand up at the window. The voices died away again. Then she lowered it. She pulled the veil off her hair. The doctor sighed and closing his eyes, this time only pretended to black out. He could hear another siren approaching. He thought it was a police car, but it could have been an ambulance. It didn't really matter which. If he could get out and throw himself on to the road, they'd stop and pick him up. By the time he had worked this out the vehicle with the siren was already passing down the street. The female opened a chink in the sacking curtain again. She looked down, but said nothing. She turned back and stared at him, disbelieving his closed eyes.

At last he heard another siren on the uptown side, coming downtown. It might take this avenue or others on each side. He had to hope that this vehicle was routed in the same way as the previous one. If he were going to make it he'd better start now. He began to unravel the doorchain. He worked fast and nervously as if saying, 'Sorry I called. You don't want to get into this, I'll go, I'm sorry,' and he almost had the chain untied when she moved.

She had observed him well. She kicked him in the side and he let out a terrible cry of pain. She swatted him, then, across the face. She didn't slap him, but struck him with the flat of her wrist and hand.

He was knocked right over. The siren came and went.

He laughed, and that surprised her. Very weakly he laughed because he couldn't tell the lie that he had only been trying to get up to go to the other end of the room. His hair wasn't so thick or long, and it was speckled with grey. She suddenly grabbed it and pulled up his head to look either at him or at the phenomenon of white laughter. He had the feeling that she had never left this district, that she would keep him as a curiosity, as a white little freak. The doctor felt thirsty. He had often seen this thirst in terminal cases and thought it came from the drugs, the morphine and heroin. But he'd had no drugs.

'Water,' he croaked. Gently, she let go of his hair and his head fell back on to his chest. She took some time to decide. Then he felt the water against his face. She was pushing his brow to lift up his head. She was looking for his cracked mouth.

She didn't seem to have a cup. So maybe she didn't usually live here. She too perhaps was on the run. She went to and from the closet, bringing water in the cup of her big hand. She must have done the journey thirty times. Then she put water over his face and head. She kept going over to the closet, then coming back and throwing the cold water at him. She tied up the chain again. Then she moved to the end of the room where the door led into the water closet. It was difficult to see what else, from the doctor's angle, but she seemed to keep her clothes in there. He could see a white plastic raincoat.

She returned with a padlock and fixed it on the big chain. As she did so the doctor looked up. His head was still on the floorboards. She was aware of his curiosity. She still didn't say a word. She didn't give him a blanket, or a cigarette. She wrapped herself up again and lay in bed smoking. After a moment or two the doctor recognized the acrid smell. She wasn't smoking tobacco; it was pot. The doctor was glad that she smoked, glad that she didn't smell like a girl.

* * *

In the distance he could still hear the sirens. They must have been police cars, maybe making inquiries, searching for weapons, making arrests. Their sounds went farther and farther away; came back, but never too near. The night went by and after a long, long while she closed her eyes. The bed was very low and he moved over towards it as imperceptibly as the grey white light of dawn stole in through the window.

* * *

He didn't know which part of her was so close; it could have been a thigh or a calf or an arm, or maybe part of her amazing trunk. He reckoned that it was hairless, that it was curiously imperfect. In a strange, waking dream the doctor reflected: Black skin isn't black at all, none of it is black. There are pores, pink pigment, shades of brown. She had a great many flaws and blemishes and creases. She smelt but she was warm.

An age after that—all time was losing its meaning—she snored and the doctor thought irritably—which is to say fearlessly—God damn it, doesn't she realize I'm dying? I'm dying of thirst.

The boards were very rough. Trying to pull himself across towards the closet he caught some splinters in his bottom and his hand. They seemed very sore. That struck him as odd. He was dying with a knife wound in his liver, and a splinter of wood felt sore. He only wanted to get to the basin. The easy way seemed to be to slide against this shiny painted wall. But he had to get up to do this, so he tried to use the chain on the door.

He tried to pull himself to his feet. The wound felt like a lump, like the swelling after a hornet's sting; incredibly sensitive and also throbbing. But the bleeding seemed to have stopped. When he pulled his cuff away from his shirt and trousers there was a little crackling noise. The blood had dried up.

He was bent in the shape of a U. He couldn't straighten up at all, not without the pain becoming intolerable. Standing like this, bent double, he still felt giddy, but he managed to push himself off with the bed, across the room to the wall, and pressing his shoulder against its painted surface he slid and shoved himself along. At the end, he saw the basin. He stepped across to it. He stumbled. He saw the china edge coming up and knew it was going to strike him on the face.

He accepted the pain. He didn't yelp any more. The water seemed too far away. He felt warmer as he passed out.

* * *

The doctor had no idea how long he was unconscious. He thought it might have been for hours, even twenty-four hours. The female was still in bed.

In fact he'd only been out for a moment or two. He'd woken to a sound — to a new and dangerous sound. Somebody had opened the front door downstairs. The doctor pulled his knees up and sheltered, pointlessly, under the basin as he heard the footsteps on the stairs. Whoever it was ran up, with a light young step. He or she might have been wearing sneakers. In a split second the doctor made several wild deductions which brought him to the conclusion that the caller was this female's boyfriend; that he was some kind of athlete, probably a boxer.

There was a knock on the door. The doctor's eyes were very bright. The female didn't move. There was another knock and a voice, a small voice said, 'It's me, Delivery.' It was a child's voice. But even a child can raise an alarm. The doctor looked at the female who was awake. Her eyes were open. She did not move.

The door hinges were the doctor's end of the room. Therefore, when the delivery boy pushed the door open until the chain and lock restrained it he could see the windows and maybe the female, through the crack, but still could not see the doctor. He pushed through a big bottle of Coke and a carton of milk.

The boy said, 'Why don't you come out today? There's been a riot. You heard? They burnt a car with all the men in it. Harry got hurt bad. He's in the hospital. His back's bust up. You got to come out tonight. Big cabaret when they come in. You don't just want to lie there and smoke pot, do you? Big drinking in Charlie's.'

She did not move. It was hard to tell the relationship between the female and the boy but it seemed the boy liked her. Yet respected her, was a little too much in awe of her to be her brother. The doctor couldn't see the boy but he thought he must be twelve at most. The arm and hand that poked through the crack delivering the bottle and the carton was thin and small and very black.

Her eyes were on the doctor, not the boy. The doctor thought, She's enjoying this. She wants to see my fear. It's a tension she enjoys.'

The boy still didn't leave. The doctor thought he was probably kneeling, or maybe sitting on his heels out there.

The boy said, 'I just come from the Rib Room. Charlie says you got to come out. Says like you need the money anyhow. Why don't you come out? Though you got a chain and lock they'll just axe it down like the cops done last time. Charlie says to tell you he got a hatchet, too. But it's good for you to come out, not just lie smoking the old pot. Please, eh?'

Still she watched the doctor and the doctor watched her.

'What you looking at?' the boy asked her. 'You wink at me, I go back to the Rib Room, tell Charlie alright. Eh?'

And she didn't move. After what seemed like an hour the boy said, 'Sometime you gotta come out,' and she closed her eyes. Then, long moments afterwards, the doctor heard the boy move. He didn't say anything more. Curiously he knocked and then his hand appeared on the door not much higher than the chain. He waggled it to and fro for a moment, not as if he were trying to break the chain, but as if he were sad: even despairing. He stood doing that for a long time, just as if there wasn't anything else for him to do all day. Then, maybe quarter of an hour later he wandered away. He went downstairs like a very young child sent out to play on a cold, cold day: dawdling all the way.

Only when he heard the street door slam did the doctor relax a little. His shoulders dropped an inch. Even that amount of movement could be heard in the room. She opened her eyes.

The doctor closed his. Waited as long as he could bear it, then opened them. Her eyes were still on him. Again he closed his and pretended to sleep. When he next opened his eyes hers were closed. Wrongly he took her to be asleep.

The wound was very tender and there was a board that creaked. But the basin after all was just above his head. He only had to shift a foot sideways, then reached up to the faucet. He began to make the move, then froze when the board creaked. Her eyes were still closed. He shifted again, then began to push himself up. He reached a twisted kind of kneeling position and then for some reason glanced back. Her eyes were wide open. But his thirst was terrible, now that he was so very close. Turning away from her he raised his arm, turned on the faucet and let out a 'Yes. Water. Yes.' He turned it and turned it. There was no water. The tap didn't work. It seemed to take him a long time to appreciate this. Then with a groan he dropped on to the floor again. He lay, too weak to cry. After a while he rolled over so that he could see her.

She was sitting up in the bed drinking the milk. One of the diamanté buttons had come away in her sleep. She had a nipple like a huge dark disc.

When she'd finished the milk she seemed to feel better. She took a mentholated cigarette. She kept the pack on the window sill and she put the milk carton and the Coke bottle there too.

The dust on the floor choked up the doctor's nostrils and mouth, making his thirst more insistent. He kept fading in and out of consciousness now. But he came round as soon as she stepped out of the bed.

Grabbing his collar and shoulders with both hands she hauled him up the room, and as he was on his belly the pain was appalling and hot as if he were being disembowelled with white-hot instruments. She left him between the door and the bed. She went around the corner of the cubicle to the water-closet.

The Coke and the milk were not far out of his reach. But it was necessary for him to haul himself up as far as the bed. He didn't really have the use of his right arm. He felt compelled to keep his hand and wrist over his wound, as if that held him together. But he grabbed the chain on the door with his left hand and pulled and struggled, and in a quick second, found himself on the bed. He had no time to pause, but even as he struggled over to the sill he thought how futile, how pathetic it was that he should go through all this for a drink when so obviously he was going to die anyway.

He didn't reach the carton or the bottle of Coke. She took him by the ankles and pulled him back so he was now half on and half off the lousy bed. He was gripping with his elbows because he thought he couldn't bear the pain of another fall. She had a tremendous strength. She seized him under the armpits and in one movement she hauled him on to the bed where he remained in a sitting position. She brought him water in the milk carton. The water came from the cistern above the water closet. Then she patiently, methodically dressed herself while the doctor, shivering with pain, began a story. He didn't know why he was telling it. And it took him a long time in the telling.

He said, 'I was in hospital. I was a patient in the same hospital where I was taught. I lay there quite ill, in bed.'

She didn't seem at all interested.

'A boy, just a child, can't have been more than nine

or ten which is a kind of heartbreaking age, this boy was in the next bed to mine.'

'He'd been burnt quite badly. A week or two before. So one night he starts to cry. One Sunday evening. I asked him why he should cry. He said, "Things are crawling out of my bandage." '

She went out, not long after that. She never showed that the story had affected her. Really, the doctor couldn't believe that she spoke any language, except that she looked at him sometimes, very slowly, almost, almost smiled. She went out in her jeans and shiny boots and plastic coat. And the doctor lay back with his eyes shut and still didn't dare to look down at his wound. That little boy's whimpering and his sweetness and life's appalling cruelty would never leave him, he thought.

* * *

He woke to find her immediately in front of him, kneeling on the floor. When he opened his eyes her huge yellow orbs were about two inches away. She woke him that way, by just staring him awake. Maybe she wondered if he were dead.

Her expression gave him no clue towards her feelings. But she had been and bought various things from the drugstore. She had a basin and some disinfectant and a sponge and a bandage and lint. She'd laid them all out on the filthy floor and seemed to have no idea whatsoever what to do with them, now. It did not occur to the doctor, until very much later, what a risk she must have taken by going into a shop in this district where a white man was known to be hiding and wounded; by daring to buy these things.

Together, so to speak, they stretched out the body of the doctor; which meant pain.

She hadn't bought any scissors. He asked her, snipping his fingers in gesture because he was never confident that she understood him. She looked at his fingers and thought. She grabbed his hand in her big hand and looked at it as if it were new to her. The doctor's was a good, sensitive hand. Then she put it to one side again as if it bored her and she wandered over to the other side of the room.

The doctor who was now laid out, knew that the straightening process had once again opened the wound. He couldn't move. He just managed to tip his neck. He saw that she was idling about, smoking a cigarette. Evidently she'd brought some provisions, too. And a paraffin stove, which was good news. It was already lit.

The doctor said, 'I'm bleeding, I think.'

She was opening a tin of peanut butter. She paused. Then she screwed it up tight again. She moved to the basin and picked up a rusty razor-blade there. She took a long drag at her cigarette, then stubbed it out. She removed her satin slippers. She gave one to the doctor and opened and closed her mouth indicating that he should bite hard.

He did not at once obey and as she began to slice away the cloth of shirt and trousers which was congealed with blood he let out a cry. She slapped his face. The slipper fell inside the bed against the wall. She burrowed underneath, knocked some of the dust off it and gave it back to him. The doctor stared at it. He stared absently at the toe of the satin slipper. He saw it was marked. Looking closer he rightly recognized blood. He supposed it to be his own. She picked up the rusty razor-blade again. It was as if, until this moment, she had decided to leave everything in the hands of God. Now something had made her decide to cope: maybe the maggots on the boy's burn.

But she didn't find it easy. The doctor could tell that from the sweat on her brow. He hardly trusted his judgments about her, she was always unpredictable, but he thought she perhaps was squeamish about the sight of blood.

He still thought that as she cut and tugged and tore, and pulled the cloth away. He had to chew the slipper all the time now as she took the sponge. He thought about the blood: how quickly it congealed. For a moment he dared to look down. There were no maggots. She shoved his face back, with her big hand.

She seemed very puzzled about the bandaging once she had laid the lint. But eventually she decided that the only possible way was round and round his waist. He arched his back a little. It took a long time but in the end the pain was easier. She had remembered to buy a safety pin.

When she had finished, she smiled; the first time he had ever seen that huge, generous golden grin:

literally golden, thanks to the gold-capped teeth. She seemed most pleased with the final pin. She seemed pleased with herself. She didn't smile at him, but at the bandage and the pin. She walked away and lit another cigarette. She smoked mentholated cigarettes.

The doctor thought that that knife, that little knife, couldn't have touched his liver or he wouldn't be alive still. It must have missed it by a fraction of an inch. Now maybe he was bleeding internally, but there was a chance of life.

She pulled a blanket over him, then put on her plastic coat and walked out.

* * *

He heard a Sinatra tune, played on some scratchy disc. When it stopped there was a short pause, then it began again: 'Come Fly With Me'. And began again and again.

She was smoking pot. He was on the end of the bed. Her toes were under his thighs; he was her hot-water bottle. Even if she saw him stir and recognized that he was awake, it seemed she wasn't interested. It was dark. She looked so contented that he dared not disturb her. He could see out of her window. The sky was quite clear. There was a moon with a frosty ring around it. He stretched to look down at the telephone kiosk. The disc ended. Then started again. They might be nearing dawn. It was very cold.

He drifted. Then the record stopped without starting again. It was a little bakelite machine that worked on batteries. She'd finished her smoke.

Quite suddenly he said, 'I used to give my daughter Lilian candies.' He had no idea what prompted him to say that out loud just like that. Some complicated defensive system; some instinct about salvation.

Then he shut up again. His mind flitted from childhood to the early days with Lilian. He didn't seem to have the concentration to stick to any memory or problem for more than a few seconds at a stretch.

She was moving her toes; moving them persistently, pressing and knocking but not quite kicking him. She didn't put them anywhere near his wound. She began to move her feet more impatiently, insistently, disturbing him.

He said, 'You've got to have a blonde daughter.'

The toes stopped. He took one. She buffeted his leg with her feet again. He nodded. He said, 'I'll tell you about Lilian.' The buffeting stopped. He couldn't remember anything about Lilian, suddenly. But he tried.

He said, 'A man who loses a wife and gains a daughter has got to hate his daughter or else love her too much. To spoil her. That's what you'd think.'

He took a long pause. Then he said, 'But that leaves out the daughter. It isn't just up to the man. I got a good one. I got one that didn't want to be spoilt. Maybe that's because she has yellow hair and a very fine straightforward kind of face. With my eyes, exactly my eyes. Lilian never needed me, she just liked me, loved me. Lilian isn't selfish, never was. She's self-whatever it is. She's composed. She's self-sufficient. She never got in my way. Some folk say we lived in parallel, that's not true. We love each other. We're a good-mannered father and daughter. She knew how her mother made me the loser, so she didn't have to ask about that. Once I started to tell her how maybe it wasn't all her mother's fault, she just put her hand over my mouth. We're the best-mannered father and daughter. We didn't go in for big scenes. She's never seen me cry and I hardly ever saw her. We lived in the doctor's house. She was very good with the patients if they rang. What a blessing Lilian was. Is.'

The doctor had run out. She waited for a while. Then she suddenly lifted up her knees and, with one big shove, pushed him right off the end of the bed. Two minutes later she was snoring, asleep.

He thought, If I could find that padlock key. It's late now. Must be the middle of the night. Only the sounds of the war in the distance. The kiosk was almost exactly opposite, not more than fifty yards. He could make that. While she snored he sat up. He looked around the place. Where would she keep the key? Maybe in the pocket of her jeans or the pocket of her coat? Maybe under her pillow? Maybe on the sill?

He started to creep around. He didn't find it in any of these places. He found something else on the sill. He found a newspaper and something about the headline caught his attention. The paper was three months old. Looking down the front page he saw how she'd marked a photograph with this big jumbo biro pen, a kind of joke pen she had. The picture was of some kind of disturbance or riot and it was in front of MISTER CHARLES'S RIB ROOM written up in lights. She'd ringed a girl fighting with the cops. The face was unrecognizable, half hidden by the police truncheons raining down on the victim: but the girl was wearing a white plastic raincoat.

Searching again for the key, even daring to put his hand under the bolster, the truth didn't occur to the doctor. Was the padlock self-locking? There was no key. Neither, now, was there a lock.

* * *

She never said a word. Occasionally she'd hum that Sinatra tune in a weird way of her own. But she had a tongue. She could laugh, too. She had the strangest sense of humour.

Waking one morning—and the doctor never knew whether it was two days or three days after—he felt altogether different. He felt stronger and it took him a moment to understand why. The sun had broken through the clouds outside. There was a noise of people and cars in the street. She must have opened the window. And as he lay watching the dust in the sunbeam that fell on to the bed and floor he felt a persistent pressure against the back of his neck. He moved a little then again felt the tickle. He didn't think what it might be. He was warm in the sun. To begin with, he had thought she was more like an animal than a woman, she slept so much, night and day, but now he had quite taken to her ways. He too slept most of the time. Then again there was a pressing against the nape of his neck.

It was her toe. Her great big toe. He looked beyond it, over the mountains and forests of the great feline body, some hilltops in the sunshine, some valleys in the dark; he saw she was leaning on one elbow, grinning at him. He remembered now. They had eaten well the night before. She had gone out and bought hot dogs and some Mexican muck and bread and milk and beer. Now she was playful. But she was always dangerous. Sometimes, as they slept, he would move towards her, because he was cold, in his sleep. She more than once shoved him right out of the bed.

Again the toe wriggled and invited games. She pushed his nose and began to chuckle when he turned away and rubbed it with his hand. The toe pushed at his shoulder. It was a powerful great toe. So he caught hold of it and tickled the sole of her foot until she began to laugh. He twisted her other foot and she rolled over, laughing. She was more or less naked in the sun. She tried to get away from being tickled now. But the doctor knew the pressure points and the nerve centres. They moved round the bed in a childish, slumbrous, ridiculous kind of way, and the doctor was calling her names, in the way that a lion-tamer called a lioness all sorts of names. The message lay in his tone which went with the lazy morning sunbeam.

At last he put his thumb in that junction of the nerve that lies between shoulder and neck. The doctor's hands were delicate, but they had strength.

That was when she really began to laugh and without her saying a word the doctor understood why, completely. She really could not believe that this old invalid could hold her down. She tried to move out of his hold and he laughed at her. He was applying pressure only with one hand but he still had her face pinned to the awful filthy striped bolster on that buggy bed. She moved her hips and legs and arms, without ever striking near his wound, but still she couldn't fight free. Eventually she became so weak with laughter that he was holding her only with his thumb.

At last he let her go. She was determined that he should teach her where exactly to apply the pressure for this old, old hold. So the doctor became the victim, and she laughed as much again when she found she could pin him down with one finger. When she let go she took hold of his hair affectionately and shook his head about. For an instant he wondered if she had broken his neck. Then they had another big meal. The doctor developed a great taste for beer. He found some dollars in his pocket and told her to buy more, but she didn't take his money. And the doctor asked her, 'Why the hell are you doing this?' At that she'd turned away.

It was the pressure point, strangely, that led to the only bad quarrel. Lord knows how many days later. They had eaten many more sausages and in the corner there were piles of beer cans. This time, it was later at night, maybe after too many beers, when she started fooling around. She pinned his head not on to the blanket but on to the floor, and it hurt. He tried to break free, but she applied the pressure much more strongly, and the pain increased. Like a boy, the doctor suddenly grew angry, and tried very hard to get free. Possibly she knew that he was in earnest and for some contrary reason continued to apply pressure.

He managed to catch her forefinger and sharply, very sharply bent it back. Not only did she release the pressure, she let out a cry and fell back in the corner by all the cans. Still angry, and swearing at her, vindictively, he slapped her face, to warn and punish her. Bitch.

She held her head to one side, as if waiting for him to strike again. She remained absolutely still. He felt afraid. He withdrew a step but did not apologize. He stood up and stared down at her. He was stronger, now, but not that strong. Besides, she still only had to call out the window and he would be dead. He knew that.

But the politics of the room had suddenly changed.

Very slowly she turned her face and stared at him, unblinkingly. He held her stare only for a moment, then, with a shrug, he turned away. He went over to the shelf where they kept the food. He said, 'Come on, there's more cheese and bread.' He said, 'Anyway you haven't finished your beer.' His voice was far from confident.

After a little while, she picked herself up and came across and drank a little. She spread some peanut butter on her bread.

The doctor was anxious to express what had happened. Also to apologize for it. He said, 'You don't know your own strength, that's the trouble. You had me half dead on the floor. Why did you want to do a thing like that?' Somehow everything he said rang false. Secretly he knew why. She might have made a mistake. But with that last blow of his—that 'Down, slave', that 'Take that and mind your manners'—he had made no mistake. He had called something up from the unforgotten past. It was therefore for him to say sorry. Yet as soon as he opened his mouth to do so, he knew he had made a mistake. He had confessed to something of which she had not previously been absolutely sure.

'Look, Cat, I'm sorry if—'

With a single swipe of her hand she removed plates, cans, knife, bread, peanut butter—the whole damned shooting match on to the floor. Everything was smashed and scattered about.

He was shaken and enraged. He stood quite still, white and trembling with anger. She watched him again. With great effort he managed to recover himself. He then said very quickly, 'You are inviting me to strike you again. I will not do so.'

She stared at him for moments on end. Then she turned away, pulled on her jeans and her big pullover; put on her plastic coat. She lit a cigarette, hummed 'Strangers in the Night', and stepping over the debris she unrolled the chain and walked out of the dump.

The doctor was still shaking. He did not attempt to tidy up. He suddenly felt desperately depressed. He climbed on to the bed, rolled a blanket round him and, white man, prayed for sleep.

The next morning broke gloomily with the sky low and overcast. Bad dreams weren't scattered away. The doctor moved her arm without waking her and stepped over her. He put on his shoes and his coat, still without waking her. He finished an open can of beer and lit one of her cigarettes. Very gently he took the chain off the door. He laid it on the floor, soundlessly. He opened the door swiftly so that it would not creak and closed it similarly, once he had stepped out into the landing.

Downstairs, in the deserted hall, he knew that he had been bluffing; had been praying that she should wake up. So it was only now that he seriously considered his escape.

He had no idea how many days had passed since the night that Angel got away, but he reckoned it must have been the best part of two weeks. The real world outside was still at this moment no more than black shadows seen through the frosted glass on the closed front door, but it frightened him. Patients, like released prisoners, first feel alarmed by reality. He'd forgotten just how much.

He thought the best plan would simply be to bluff it out. Just walk out there, clap his hands, yell 'Taxi'.

He felt quite unreal as he stepped outside. The door banged behind him. He was scared that it had locked but did not dare hesitate now. He had forgotten the coldness of the wind. It was still coming across the frozen lake. It hit him very hard and took his breath away. Buttoning up, he looked left and right and thought he saw some kind of junction two or three blocks up to the right. He would find a taxi there.

At the first crossing, just as he was about to step off the island towards the sidewalk on the far side he looked up and caught a man's eye. That man knew him. Whether he was posted there the doctor never knew. He emerged from a doorway and looked. The doctor panicked, at once. There was only one white man in the world.

The doctor was almost run over by a truck as he ran back. He darted and dodged through the coloured men and women struggling up the street against the wind. They must have heard a shout, but most of them were too cold to appreciate its meaning, fast enough.

The doctor found the door. It wasn't locked. He banged it shut behind him. He rushed upstairs, like a frightened schoolboy: Mummy, Mummy. When he came to the landing he flung open the door. In the space of five seconds, without any words, the pair of them exchanged two chapters.

She was up. She was dressed. She was tidying up. She was half smiling as if to say, 'I knew you were only bluffing going downstairs and banging the door like that, old man, but I too am sorry about last night. I've thought, and you're right. I was provoking you to behave like a white man, but now we can forget it. I want to forget it, that's why I'm doing this thing for you. That's why I'm tidying up the joint.'

And he was saying, 'Cat, no. No. I've gone and torn it. I must have been crazy. You made me feel so safe I got proud. I went out. I didn't bluff. I went out and they've seen me.' He said out loud, 'They're coming.' And there was the sound of voices, of several men coming together in the street down below.

The black panther is a remarkable animal.

The doctor knew that: knew about panthers and cheetahs and leopards. He'd had quite an obsession about them all his life. He'd always loved animals and the cats, the cat family intrigued him most of all.

These feline animals never run in the way people imagine them to do. They leap and bound forward a little faster than the eye can accurately follow. But they can't run for long. Not like a dog or a deer. For an instant their power seems to be limitless, its speed infinite. But they can't run at all.

She took the stairs to the second floor in two bounds. She grabbed the doctor's hand and pulled him up the next flight as together they heard the front door bang, below. When he stumbled, she yanked him to his feet. She leapt up into an attic area, and pulled him up behind her with both hands. She crashed through a door on to the flat roof. She didn't give the doctor time to grow giddy. She leapt from one roof to the next over chasms that dropped five storeys to the street. It was icy and slippery.

But in all, they didn't cover more than half the block. She opened a skylight. The roofs seemed to be a world she knew. She dropped through the skylight and the doctor tumbled after. At once, again, she pulled him to his feet. She closed the skylight. She took the first six or seven down steps in a bound. The doctor rattled behind. Then the next. They passed like this through a house filled with astonished mothers and children, most of whom seemed to be oriental. They simply saw the flash of white plastic coat and the doctor, banana legged, falling behind.

Then they were in a street of dilapidated redstone houses with steps up to each front door. There were still piles of frozen snow, but it was brown and doggy now. At this stage the doctor could have taken over the lead. The cat can't run. When she stopped at the seventh house he thought she was pausing for breath. He urged her on.

But she had some plan. She looked all the way round. The whole environment, every detail of it from the roof to the ash-can blown in the wind was contained, for an instant, in those unblinking, yellow eyes.

Suddenly she took the doctor's hand and strode across the street to a house that was labelled DENTAL SURGEON.

The house had a double door. The first was unlocked. Inside were the bells for the different apartments. She pressed 'Consulting Room' and hummed uneasily as she waited. The doctor had his hand over his side. He was bent forward, trying to regain his breath. The inner door was glazed. The glass plate rattled as the nurse opened it. It rattled again as the nurse was flung aside. She protested too late. The fugitives had arrived. Even the doctor was learning to react fast, like that.

The dentist's waiting-room was dingy and yet also

tawdry with touches of red and gold on curtains and carpet. It was not very clean.

The nurse went to fetch the dentist, who wasn't next door in the surgery, but upstairs, in his apartment, drinking hot soup. It must have been about 11.00 a.m. and he hadn't seen any patients yet. Meantime, the doctor half sat and half lay on a greasy upholstered sofa while his saviour paced up and down and round the room, much like an athlete infuriated by an unjust decision at the finish of a race.

In crisis, some men, especially frightened men, seem to speak in code. Or maybe some know no other language. They have to approximate their actual reaction to archetypal form. The coloured dentist was thin with horn-rimmed glasses. His clothes didn't seem to fit him too well. His wrists stuck out of his white coat. His trousers were too short.

He called her by the name the doctor had never heard. It was such an obvious name. He said, 'Silence, honey, you can't do this to me, Silence. You got to go. You can't stay here. You know it. That's not fair to me or mine, baby. Silence, you got to be on your way.'

She looked down at him and waited until he stopped. Then she led the way into the surgery. They closed the door behind them, leaving the doctor out.

The doctor could not then hear what the dentist said. He could pick up the perturbed, insistent, not too persuasive tone but he was missing the words, even when he crossed to the door to try to learn more.

The doctor was not at all sure where the dentist stood. He had noticed only one thing: the dentist had behaved as if Silence were on her own. He had not acknowledged the doctor's presence at all, not by the bat of an eyelid. It was as if he were already preparing his testimony to some Moslem inquisition: 'Sure, Silence came round, but I never saw anybody with her. I saw nobody else, at all.'

The doctor thought he heard Silence moan in a strange way, but the sound was not repeated, so soon he came away from the door. The waiting-room had some kind of central heating which did not make him feel more confident. It worried him after the cold: even made him feel a little sick. And he was troubled with the wound. He had stuffed his dirty handkerchief into place over the ruckled bandage underneath his belt. He dreaded that the wound had opened again. But he stuck his finger down the bandage and there was no redness. Just sweat.

He sat back.

It took him half a minute to recognize the picture which was not a photograph but a painting on the cover of a weekly news magazine. It was lying on the table in front of his eyes. His daughter Lilian was where all the pretty girls hope one day to be; in glorious colour, on the cover. And underneath there was a caption: 'The girl it's all about.'

It frightened the doctor. He hardly dared open the magazine. He suddenly didn't want to know. He felt that there were only bad things to be learnt. It wasn't that he wanted simply not to read the magazine: he wanted the magazine and the story never to have been. Suddenly he didn't want to see Lilian again. He didn't want to go home, ever. He wanted to be back in the room that smelt of paraffin, the room that was newly tidied up. And he knew how much he had been fighting to bury the truth. Just as he had avoided all inquiry about his son, his son also was there in front of him, staring at him. He thought, I cannot read it, even as his eye started down the page. The story occupied three, nearly four pages. It was the national lead.

Angel had got back to tell his version, which wasn't too untrue. But the doctor couldn't read it. He turned over the page and there were pictures of himself and Angel and Junior, and of the coloured boy who was dead. The doctor took that in. He still kept skipping the lines about Junior.

Junior wasn't his only son, he was just the one most likely to succeed. Throughout his school career other men and women used to stop the doctor in the street and say, 'Boy but you've got a winner there.' Junior played football, came top of the class. A fine boy, doctor. A fine, unsmiling young God who always made the grade.

There was another photograph which suddenly took the doctor's attention. It was a horrible blown-up snapshot of Silence. She had dark hair cut quite short and it gave no impression of her size nor her dignity. Her eyes looked brown. The caption underneath the picture said, 'Silence is black,' in the funny, punning way that magazines favour. The doctor read the paragraph about her. She had a previous record of crime;

also of crime with violence. She was one of five coloured men and women whom the police were anxious to interview concerning the murder by lynching in the street, two days after 'the battle', of Lawrence Ewing Junior.

The doctor began to shake. He closed the magazine, again. He had somehow already, magically, picked up the truth. He had read the whole article while he pretended not to, and he was left with one blazing impression on his mind. It was of a satin slipper with his son's blood.

He tried to make himself open the paper again and read all the things not only that the newsmen had reported but what important politicians and international commentators had said. He closed the pages yet again. He began to feel very shivery and weird, then knew suddenly that he was going to be sick. He needed somewhere to vomit. The surgery would have a basin. He rushed through, caught sight of the basin, ran to it and retched; then retched again.

When he recovered he saw that there was nobody in the room. This frightened him more, because his fear was running ahead of his reasoning again. It seemed to be the exposure, the sheer exposure of the story, the simple horror of being involved in all this that most frightened him. His mind would not settle on any particular aspect: on the death of the child; on Silence's actions; on Junior's death; on the dentist's panic; on the sudden disappearance of both the dentist and Silence. Somehow the magazine itself became the object of terror for him. He felt the whole world to be against him; black and white. The doctor knew his physical condition had something to do with it. He recognized in himself some kind of shock but he could not separate the true reason behind it yet. He just didn't have the energy to be brave. He didn't even want to cry. There simply wasn't anywhere in the world to go, he felt, where there would be safety. Nowhere, except to Silence.

As he picked up the magazine again, there was a noise at the front door. He threw the paper away. He wanted to hide. Then he guessed that somebody was leaving, not arriving.

Very frightened, he tiptoed to the window, and peeping through the side of the curtain, looked down at the street a few feet away, below.

The dentist and his wife and children were getting into their Chevrolet. They seemed to have come downstairs and left the building unnaturally quietly, but now in the street, the dentist seemed anxious to convey the impression that he was starting on a normal family outing, maybe going to the movies, or the ball game, or even a prayer meeting. The dentist was wearing a strangely formal hat with a broad brim, almost like a Dutch Protestant's. He had to hold on to it, in the wind. It is extraordinary which detail the mind retains.

The doctor should have been able to deduce certain things from his departure. He could not bring his mind to bear on the problems logically any more. The doctor wasn't coping very well.

* * *

Not well at all. The doctor had often seen patients in the strange state of mind which he had now reached. Usually they were widows who had lost, or felt that they had lost all incentive to live. They operated with extreme inefficiency, constantly busy, but achieving nothing. It was a phenomenon the doctor always watched very carefully, because unless checked it developed into total breakdown or withdrawal. The widow's mind became fixed upon her husband's last sickness or the moment of death. The doctor could not take his mind off the satin slipper and the pencilled ring on the photograph he had seen in her paper which had seemed to be of a lynching.

He wandered back into the surgery. He took up the magazine again and read it now, dully, as if it concerned some other family. Yes, the coloured boy had broken his spine. He had died the next day. Yes, Lawrence Ewing Junior had been discovered two days after the battle and had been killed by the mob before the police arrived on the spot. Yes, Angel had given a full and honest account of the whole affair. Doctor Ewing himself was reported to be badly wounded, and few people believed him still alive.

In the dentist's drawer, there were some surgical instruments, including a very small sharp knife with a blade even thinner than the one which the doctor had seen for an instant as it passed into his side. The handle of the dentist's knife was steel. Because it didn't fold, the doctor wrapped the blade round with some cotton wool, then he placed it in his breast pocket, diagonally, so that it didn't show.

The doctor wasn't coping very well. He knew he was incapable of killing anybody else with that knife. He knew he had no intentions of killing himself. It was a pointless acquisition which still he seemed to need.

Then, from the waiting-room he picked up another magazine. This one also had a full report on the 'Lilian' affair. But this was a coloured weekly for coloured people. More accurately, a semi-coloured weekly for those coloured people who wanted to enjoy the privileges of the white. The advertisements showed girls with straight smooth hair and firm, straight noses. The doctor looked at the articles in it with vague dismay. They were nauseating. They had nothing to do with Silence and nothing to do with him. Yet he read on, for a while, sitting in the dentist's chair.

The chair itself was modern. Perhaps dentists can hire them. The rest of the equipment looked old and not even clean.

He began to think that perhaps the dentist had persuaded Silence to leave him. There was logic in that he could see. She had every reason to fear the police but no reason to fear her own people, so long as she remained alone. To them she was no traitor. But seen with him, father of the man she had helped to murder, she was an enemy of the coloured people. The doctor thought, I never before wanted to fall into the hands of the police. I do now. Badly.

The doctor was still sitting, frozen, when he heard the front door open and close. He stood up, like an old man and stared through the open door into the other room, waiting for he did not know what.

When she walked in, he thought, I shan't mention to her that she murdered my son. He thought that quite undramatically much as if he were at home when his mother called round unexpectedly: I shan't tell her I have a toothache, it will only involve us in an unnecessary scene.

* * *

It wasn't easy to bluff Silence. Because she had dismissed words altogether her visual sense was astonishingly acute. She could see the shadow of a shade. She could read the tiniest movement of the lines round the doctor's eyes and mouth. She could see his hands tremble inside his coat pockets. The doctor therefore could not recover the subsequent situation. The more he protested, in order to save her feelings, the less he persuaded her.

She had been out. She had been to the shops. She had bought herself an exotic new dress and some fantastic costume jewelry, not in order to impress the doctor, but to please him; he knew that. And she looked just awful: so bad that she came to resemble some of the hybrids in that vulgar magazine which the doctor had left on the floor by the dentist's chair.

The doctor had come to admire her looks when she was naked or in her jeans and pullover. He didn't know if he desired her. Possibly he did. Does a child desire the mother? Not that she was purely mother.

The circumstances were not such that he then had to answer that. Perhaps he didn't have the courage to desire her. The doctor was a modest man and over forty years old.

She quite broke down; collapsed like the wife in a bad domestic comedy, the one who has spent the housekeeping money on an ugly mink hat. The doctor reassured her in vain. She tugged off her earrings, hurting herself; she threw them into the corner of the mangy waiting-room.

The doctor took off his overcoat, as if he were prepared to spend some hours convincing her that she had spent her money well.

What a strange farce, the doctor thought; how odd is reality; does she also know that she murdered Lawrence my son?

She moved into the surgery, carrying her parcels with her. The doctor followed. While she was a goddess she was also always a child. She tore open one paper shopping bag, tore it and threw her jeans and pullover across the linoleum floor. She had decided to change. The doctor kept saying, 'No, don't please,' but nothing would stop her. She was unzipping the new dress.

'Silence, don't. Really I like it,' the doctor said, then both, for an instant, froze. He had never used her name before. Both minds moved swiftly, in exact parallel. Both had the alibi. Both knew that the dentist had called her Silence. Both also knew that he had learnt 'Silence' from the press. But both had the alibi.

The zip stuck. She wouldn't let him help. She tore the dress. Ripped it and stepped out of it. Really, no grown-up white girl could have changed her clothes like this, not even if she were with her lover. Still angry, she paced round like a huffy ten-year-old, in pants, but for some reason without a bra. Then she hauled on her jeans and got lost in her sweater which should have been unbuttoned before she tried to pull it over her big head.

The performance quite humanized the doctor. He laughed and at last she let him help. But she didn't laugh herself. She was still too deeply disappointed and offended. When he tried to hold on to her, once the sweater was buttoned at the neck, she moved away. What a body it was. She could bend and pick something off the floor without even dipping her knees. It was one of the magazines she picked up. The white one, so to speak. She strutted next door. She closed the curtains against the dull day and the world that was full of their enemies. She switched on the overhead light which had a cheap shade to make it look like a Japanese lantern.

Silence never sat in an orderly way. Now she sprawled on the floor on her stomach, and began to turn over the pages. She was looking at the lead article; of course she was. She read it as if it bored her slightly, as if it had nothing whatsoever to do with the two of them. The doctor sat on the greasy sofa, watching her. He took one of her cigarettes which she put on the floor close to his feet. Only when she turned over the page, did he say, 'It's not a very good photograph of you. I wouldn't have recognized you.'

She tipped up her head. For some reason he expected her to grin. Perhaps the very way that she lifted her head made him sure that she was glad he thought it was a lousy photograph too. But her expression was utterly different. It was blank and hostile, and yet tears were running down her cheeks. That was her confession. He could see that. It caught him unawares. He began to sway backwards and forwards, like a lean little bear; a very unhappy, cornered animal of some sort. She'd forced the moment on him. It was no longer possible to avoid the issue. He felt stuck; completely stuck. She never took her yellow eyes off him, waiting for his judgment. Even morally, the doctor thought, I am a coward and she is brave.

'Shock,' he said out loud, at last. 'Shock. Just a state of shock.'

He smoked half the cigarette, but she still stared. Still she wouldn't let him off the hook. She was frowning now, deeply, as if she were afraid that he would disappoint her. How little we need words, the doctor thought.

'Shocked by the terrible truth,' he said very quietly. 'Shocked by how little I care that my own son is dead.'

He looked up as if to ask her reassurance and help. Her reaction was neutral. It was as if she could not quite accept what he said. She was staring at him, her eyes less wide open than usual.

'He seemed very separate once he was grown up,'

the doctor said flatly. 'But I didn't know how separate.' Still she looked dissatisfied. The doctor was beginning to tremble badly. To tremble unexpectedly and very violently. To tremble as it were, at the foundations, which is to say in those ditches of life where we find the meetings of mothers and daughters, of fathers and sons.

She sat. She laid her big hand on his knee. He continued to smoke and shake like a leaf. He looked only at her hand and touched a finger of it, saying, 'God knows why you paint one nail red.' Then almost without a break he continued, 'Why did you take such a vow, who tortured you, or am I wrong? Can't you speak? Is it your throat? I know you have a tongue. What terrible event moved you to take such a desperate protest? If you can talk, talk now.'

He looked up and saw only the top of her head. The black hair grew beneath the dry brown. She was lighting herself a cigarette. He said, 'I didn't feel at all. When I knew about the boy I didn't feel anything. That was the shock. Maybe I guessed ten days ago. I can't see why you've saved me. You've only seen the worst in me. The coward in me. You've seen nothing in me. I wish we'd never left that ghastly hovel. I didn't feel anything for him. I couldn't find Absalom. That is why I shake.'

He heard her say, 'Shsh.' Say, 'Shsh,' again. But she wouldn't speak. They waited like that for a moment or two, both smoking again.

He asked, 'Did you say out loud to somebody— did you say to some Court? Did you say "I'll never speak again"?' He turned her face up and she smiled quite mildly and he saw her beauty as he had never recognized it before. It was sculptured and strong and not aggressive at all. He asked, 'Or did you say it two hundred years ago?'

She turned away, but he insisted, as if it helped him to stop trembling. He said, 'We can't get away from slavery,' and bent and kissed her hand which she then withdrew. She was beginning to grow very restless. He used her name in a strange way. He said, 'In Silence's company, slavery was yesterday. If I get through, I'll tell them only that. But I can't show you how strongly I feel it. I see you often on some African coast, herded on board a crowded ship amongst the shouting and wailing and noise of despair. There is a staggering strength in your silence. Believe me, the most magnificent pathetic protest of them all.'

She began to sway as if caged. To pull away. But he held on to her wrist very hard. He spoke in a most unusually animated way as if it had to be said. 'You decided on this silence, complete, utter, unbroken. Alone, standing alone on board this terrible ship as it pulled away from the quay. Give me one word. Say "yes". Say, "Yes, you're right, that's when I decided not to speak."'

She broke away. Began to hum some unrecognizable tune. She moved like an animal, swiftly and smoothly. She had taken off her boots. She went to the surgery and brought back one of her parcels. She grinned and spun round as if to say 'Party, party!' She had bought Coca Cola and rum.

And the doctor thought, How strange it is, but if you know that you're not going to get any answer you begin to stop asking about the future. There was no point in his asking, 'What happened to the dentist?' No point in saying, 'You were in there while he talked to you for half an hour, so what did he say? I heard you moan.' No point in inquiring, 'Where do we go from here?' For she lived in the present, she lived for now as if she alone understood the immediacy and magnitude of the war.

The spirit steadied the doctor considerably. How quickly moods change in crisis. Not hers, but his. The liquor went straight to his head. The doctor soon could envisage a moment in which his behaviour could be called something like heroic. The doctor thought, Half the battle is won if you see yourself being brave.

She got drunk, too. Drunk enough to show him suddenly a big gap in her front teeth. Then only did he begin to understand their present circumstances. All the gold had gone, and that was a lot of gold. Several teeth had been capped that way. The gold must have paid for more than rum and Coke.

The doctor was beginning to cope again, beginning to be able to connect ideas, to build the chains which alone keep us sane; to link cause and effect. The dentist had extracted the gold, then she had gone out shopping. Maybe she had also paid the dentist for the apartment. He could have needed cash. He certainly didn't have many customers. Then, Maybe it's Sunday, the doctor thought. For a second his mind flitted home to Sunday and church and boredom and belief: to telling the children the right things, how to behave ...

Lawrence Junior dead.

She grew hopelessly, helplessly drunk. She laughed and hummed and danced about. She slipped, fell, knocked things over and invited the doctor to jive or twist or whatever it was. She had no head for liquor at all. She must have known that.

She also was sick in the surgery basin, but that didn't hold her back for too long. It simply revealed what he knew, namely that she wasn't happy at all. Revealed what they both knew, namely that neither of them felt any joy. He helped her back into the waiting-room and put a cushion under her head. It wasn't exactly a cushion, but the back pad of the only easy-chair. One of the springs was piercing through. She indicated that the world was going round and round, then began to look very green.

When she closed her eyes the doctor returned to the surgery and put an inch of water in a tumbler full of rum. He vowed he'd never again go to Angel's club without first drinking a full tumbler of rum.

* * *

The telephone rang. Thinking she was still incapably drunk, the doctor tried to prevent her from removing the receiver from the rest. She gave him one of those blows with the inside of the wrist. She caught him very hard, just over the right eye, and, rum-logged, he still felt the pain.

It was the dentist on the line. It wasn't the voice but the phoney smooth phrases, the 'honeys' and 'babies' that made the doctor sure.

The instrument was attached to the surgery wall. Silence stood cross-legged as if she were listening to some idle gossip and she never opened her mouth. At the end she simply hung up. The doctor wondered how the dentist could have been confident that he was speaking to her in the first place. Yet if I'd rung Silence, the doctor thought, I'd have known. Which sounds ridiculous but still was true: he'd have felt Silence at the end of the phone.

The message was perfectly simple. A price had been accepted. The dentist had handed over a pack of dollars to some intermediary character and it was up to the doctor to complete payment when he arrived safely in Whitesville; uptown. The dentist referred to the doctor as 'the passenger', which had style. The driver was to come to the house after dark, at exactly ten.

She'd bought some food; some awful Chinese food, this time, in foil-lined cartons. The doctor obligingly ate in the surgery, but he never could bluff her. Seeing that he was not enjoying the food she soon moved away and lay down in the waiting-room again.

He didn't ask her to come close this last hour. He sat on the sofa and soon she went back to him. She laid her head on his lap not just because she felt tired and a little sick. The only thing he said in that long, long hour of no war was, 'Even lose your front teeth, for God's sake. You silly big bitch.' She smiled at the tone, not the words.

She was still asleep when the taxi drew up outside and the man came up the steps. But as he pressed the bell, a split instant before it rang, there were eyes—yellow eyes, blazing, unblinking, awake, aware, taking in the shadowy red room.

The bell rang.

She moved swiftly into the surgery. She grabbed a white coat, a dirty white cotton coat which was hanging behind the door. She insisted that he wear it and carry his own. She shoved notes, a hundred dollar notes into his hand.

'Aren't you coming?'

Yellow eyes.

'Not even to the door?'

There was no war at that given moment, no colour at all; just the mutual danger and alarm as the bell rang once more.

She dropped her head. He put his hand out and touched her face. Her cheeks were quite dry. She didn't raise her head again. She was standing by the dentist's chair: that's where he saw her, standing immediately beside the hydraulic chair.

The doctor said, 'Take care.'

He left the surgery, the waiting-room, the hall. There was nobody on the doorstep but the taxi double-parked in the street below. Some other car had filled the dentist's place. The taxi-driver leant back and opened the back door. It wasn't too light which helped and the doctor kept his head bent low. His courage had been at a lower ebb. Perhaps the dollars in his pocket helped: they often do.

As soon as he was in the car the driver started away. He just seemed like a rude, impatient boy.

They'd gone about three blocks. Then this boy, the driver said, 'Move over to the left.'

The doctor didn't catch it. In truth his mind had remained beside the dentist's chair. He was as calm or as silly as that. So many moods in peril.

'Move over the seat.'

The boy's voice was hostile but most city cabmen's voices seemed to the doctor unfriendly like that. He still did not grasp the danger he was in. He thought that the boy wanted him to move over because he was obstructing the view from the driver's mirror. He therefore said, 'Sorry', as he shifted across.

The boy then reached in the pocket of the car and the doctor's blood froze. Again his instinct seemed to leap ahead of reason. His spine knew that the boy had reached for a gun.

He met the boy's eye in the driving mirror. The boy had big whites to his eyes. As the car drew up at a crossing the boy said, 'You're no fucking dentist.'

The doctor was still coping. He was scared but he was still making those necessary links. He thought, If I show him the dollar notes at this point, he'll only take them. He thought, Say nothing, doctor, if there's nothing to say.

The lights changed. The boy drove forward again.

They were on the lakeside, the doctor was sure of that, on the lakeside driving north, which was the direction in which he wanted to travel, but there was still a long long way to go. The roads were icy but the sky seemed to be clear.

The boy was driving very fast, as if he wanted to confuse his passenger. Left. Right and right again. Yet they never reached the lakeside highway. They didn't get as far as that. The boy evidently knew that the doctor was due to pay him a hundred, uptown. And maybe he had worked out what the doctor was thinking about. Suddenly he spoke.

'I don't want your money,' he said.

He never added, 'Whitey' or 'scum' or whatever. He had put on driving glasses now, which were tinted blue. They acted as a mask. But he kept watching the doctor in the mirror.

'Don't piss yourself in my cab,' he said, and so gave the doctor an important link.

The doctor's wound, for some reason, had begun to throb. Maybe the rush of adrenalin had some strange indirect influence on the pulses there. Not that the doctor cared about that. He found the throbbing reassuring. He'd been hurt before and was still living to tell the tale. Boy, he thought, if you think I look frightened, you should have seen me earlier on. The doctor was coping better. He was observing well. The streets were much emptier now. The boy despised him. 'At the next crossing, you start running,' he said.

The doctor thought to himself, What a sporting boy. Not going to shoot a sitting white bird?

The car came very suddenly to a halt. But the doctor was getting a lot, lot better. He did not crumple forward as the boy had hoped. He already had his hand on the door handle. As the car stopped he therefore catapulted straight on to the road. He somersaulted more or less, and began running almost before he found his feet. Fortunately there was no traffic coming the other way. He reached the opposite sidewalk before a truck came by.

He didn't look back. He didn't want to know if the boy was cruising after him. He ran, turned right, and ran. At the next corner he was pretty sure that he was not being followed. He had turned up a one-way lane and the boy would have had to speed round another block or else leave his car and chase on foot. There was so sign of him.

The doctor was doing better. He ran back up the block and at the next corner took the decision of his life. He turned right again. His body had seemed to take the decision for him. In moments of courage as in moments of fear, we're no longer controlled by our heads. The doctor slackened his pace. He walked. He wasn't running away.

He reckoned he should now be approaching the crossing at which the boy had dumped him. The white coat, by the way, was a stroke of genius. It was possible to walk and run in it without arousing suspicion. At the worst, the doctor thought, I can say, 'Baby', or 'Accident', or, 'I'm a doctor pretending to be a doctor, get out of my road!'

He wondered if maybe he should always drink rum. But then he had to stop for a second. He had something more than a stitch. As he bent to regain his breath he saw a little mark on the coat. The wound must have burst open somehow. It was wet and red again. Still he didn't lose his nerve. He kept thinking of these strange, almost witty things. He said to himself as he started to run again, 'Why doctor, you're a doctor running to your own emergency.'

And he wasn't running north. He had re-orientated himself and was running back into the ghetto, the idiot. He laughed at himself as he ran and walked and ran again: a left at the second crossing, then there was a warehouse, then a right.

There was no sign of the taxi, but as he ran the doctor thought about the boy. The boy was a genuine cabman, the doctor felt sure of that. The way the boy had said 'my cab' – 'Don't piss in my cab' – convinced him so. And the boy wasn't an ordinary crook, else he would have seen to it that he grabbed the hundred bucks before he lost his passenger. The boy wasn't corruptible, the doctor knew. Instinctively he hadn't tried any bribes, knowing from the boy's face that they wouldn't work. The boy had a gun. It seemed to follow that the boy was a boy with a cause and the doctor knew very well what kind of cause that might be.

So he turned his thoughts to Silence and her situation. Doing so he was beginning to discover why he was heading back that way. Silence, in the boy's eyes, must be a traitor to the cause. She had harboured the man he knew to be 'no fucking dentist'. She had harboured a man wanted by the members of this cause. Moreover, what was doubly dangerous, she had been involved with the members of this cause. She was herself wanted by the police and presumably therefore protected by the members of the cause. In their eyes she had therefore double-crossed the cause. No wonder the dentist had fled.

It would take the doctor about twenty minutes to reach the dentist's house, he thought, so long as he took no wrong turn. At least he had the dentist's knife.

When he reached the street he paused. His legs were feeling very weak. Then looking along the dim row of houses he couldn't find the dentist's surgery sign. It had been painted on a globe light shade. Indeed the more he looked at the street, the less confident did he feel. The situation was nightmarish. He was at the end of the right street. He knew he had taken no wrong turning. Yet it wasn't the same street. Hardly any cars were parked in it. There weren't any lights in the windows any more. There was nobody to be seen. Not a car. It was a ghost street. He felt as bewildered as scared. Slowly he walked along.

There wasn't a dentist's sign because it had been stoned. There weren't any dentist's windows because they had been smashed. The lace curtains swung about in the gaping space like ignominious white flags. The doctor felt the crunch of broken glass under his feet. He was being watched. He was sure of that. He turned round sharply, but nobody was there. Yet he was being watched. Not watched by one pair of eyes, the doctor thought, but by a hundred or more. The lights might be out but the people were still in their houses. Maybe the sight of a couple of shadows made the doctor sure of that: something did.

At the limit, courage closely resembles cowardice. It has its own motor: Go-man-go or Run-man-run. The doctor looked tense but composed as he stepped up then walked straight into the house.

She was naked. They may have gang-banged her first, but probably not. Nobody will ever know. She was standing, or almost standing, stark naked. Her back was like an uncooked steak that had been thrashed by a tennis racket strung with wire.

And the doctor thought, Maybe it *is* Sunday, but there is no longer any belief. So help me, they didn't do as much to Christ.

Yes, it could be called standing. She was bowed, but she was on her feet, not her knees, exactly between the waiting-room and the surgery, in the doorway. She was making absolutely no sound. Not a moan. No sound at all.

'It's me,' the doctor said. 'I've come for you. You knew I would. Show me your face. I don't care what they've done to it, show me your eyes.'

She must have been at the limit of consciousness, because when she turned round he thought for an appalling second that they had taken her eyes. The whites only were showing. But that wasn't true. She came back. The yellow eyes returned, but they were empty of all expression.

Her face could have been worse. It was bruised, smudged and scratched but it wasn't so bad.

Then the doctor saw that she wasn't tied to the door as at first he'd thought. Her hands weren't tied there, just a few inches above her big head. They were nailed. Nailed to the lintel with one big square nail.

'God,' the doctor murmured, 'they won't have left me any tools.' But somehow he got it out. With his bare hands. As he put it in his pocket, he thought, I want it in my grave, I do. He was holding her up now, dragging her into the surgery. The doctor could never have used the little knife, but when she lost consciousness he thought, If I had a gun I would shoot her in the temple now, because there is a god; there is a careless god. So bloody careless he makes us in his own hopelessly split image and Silence here pays in pain.

The doctor was aware that his courage was no longer coming from the money or the rum. It was coming from an historic horror: man's enslavement of man. It was an indomitable courage, a bitter courage now. He had the energy of guilt. For a second she woke. But she did not recognize him. Even his face was changed.

The dentist had been right to leave. His chair was torn from its moorings, his instruments and files scattered all over the floor. Not an hour had gone by since the boy told the doctor, 'You're no fucking dentist.' Communications have grown to be very fast in the slowest, surest war of all: the one that some merchants started when they pulled the boats away from the African and Island coasts.

Water for her. 'Christ,' he said, 'it's in our hands, not yours, not God's.' He told Silence. 'You kept *me* parched, you big black. Tip your head back now.' And in his hand, because all the vessels were smashed, he brought water from the tap in the corner to the place by the door where she lay. He must have made the journey twenty or thirty times. 'Don't you want to sit up. Not even now? Don't want to sit, don't want to talk? Don't you want to say one word to me now?'

Not that his own words mattered any more. The tone did. The tone was not so arrogant as to give confidence. It promised no relief. But he said with every breath, I'm not going to go, I'm not going to leave you, not ever, not until the end. 'So kneel, okay, kneel if that's better for the pain, kneel, or get on all fours you big cow, why the hell did you do this for me?' And he thought, Maybe it is only in our impossible love for each other that we can defeat the carelessness of God.

'We have to put something over your shoulders,' he said and she watched him as he took off his shirt. He said, 'It's damned cold outside but I'll wear your sweater, I'd like to do that.'

She shied away from him only for a second, but he caught her by the arm. She was sitting on her heels now. He said, 'We have to put something over your back because of that boy in hospital, the one with the burns. We got to cover the wound because we don't want things crawling out of the bandage.' She stayed absolutely still and he opened up the shirt. Just before he put it round her he thought, Woman, we need a sculptor to catch you sitting on your heels, waiting for more pain. For here is the result of the power and the glory of God and the indelible cruelty of man.

She hardly flinched. Out loud he said, 'Oh dear,

why did I find myself such a big moose, why did I ever take that particular door? Look, you know who I am. Idiot, I came back. Now big animal, get up on your feet. Please get up on your feet. Oh my darling Silence, help me to help you to stand.'

They found her jeans. They found no boots. That bit wasn't so hard. They even found a beautiful, ironic mouthful of rum. She put the white coat on, this time. He took the sweater. She was standing now with her bleeding hands held straight in front of her. The doctor saw that something had to be done about them. He could see no bandage, though there was plenty of cotton wool. There was also some mild disinfectant, normally used for mouthwash. The doctor filled a basin and diluted the disinfectant. She obeyed him absolutely now. He pulled her over to the basin by her wrists and dipped her hands in the water. It evidently wasn't so painful as she had expected.

By the basin the doctor found a big pair of rubber gloves. He wished Silence's hands were smaller, because he could have packed the gloves with cotton wool. But he managed some sort of covering to the wounds with lint and wool dipped in the same disinfectant, then as gently as he could, stretching the gloves open with his own slim strong fingers, he pulled them over her hands.

So now she was in jeans, shirt, a white surgery coat and red rubber gloves. He put her plastic coat over all that, buttoning it like a cloak. He found a scarf belonging either to the dentist or some patient who had left it behind. He tied that round her neck. He had her sweater, his torn trousers and his coat turned up at the collar. But she looked round for something and he saw she was barefoot. 'I suppose you want your Cinderella slippers? Christ, that's really you. A moment like this when I'm calling forth the saints and you've got to have your horrible spangled slippers!' He found them for her and she even looked a little content. He smiled and said, 'We're a couple of swells.' She just looked at him: and looked. He pressed her arm very gently. He said, 'And we'll walk up the avenue, yes, we'll walk up the avenue.'

He took her out by the elbow. It was as if she couldn't believe a return of the love which she had never been able to explain in herself: that's how she stared at him.

* * *

Enemies, meaning people, frightened people could have been waiting outside with stones or guns. The wind had come up. The doctor and Silence both felt it hard and cold as they took the first few steps. Shakily they stepped down to the sidewalk and paused for a second in the iciness, their feet on frosted snow and broken glass.

The wind seemed to freeze the doctor's tired face. He'd put on his spectacles for some reason as they came out of the door. Perhaps he thought the lenses would give him some protection. The lines on his face looked very deep in the street light. Beside his, her face looked rounded and smooth in pain. The doctor looked all the way round the houses. Perhaps that's why he put his glasses on. But he didn't need them. He could feel that the night was filled with eyes.

His own family wouldn't have recognized the doctor now. They never knew he had a temper as terrible as this. He yelled at the windows which only appeared to be empty. 'Thank God. Oh yes. Thank God there are thousands of eyes upon us now!'

And as they walked down the street, heads appeared at the windows behind them, the onlookers gradually becoming less cautious. None of them tried to stop the couple and none of them offered to help.

Lord knows how she managed to walk. She rose to the occasion. She was too confused probably to think exactly what their walk might mean to those who saw it. She was amazed still that the doctor had come back to her, pulled her back from death. Maybe surprised that nobody shot at them. Nobody threw a single stone. They walked with more and more confidence until they were both almost straight-backed, like an ancient couple determined not to reveal their infirmities. Look what's become of Adam and Eve; that's what the doctor thought.

So the eyes dwindled away. And the wind blew across this strange couple. It blew hard and cold across the lake, until there were no longer any eyes. Even the stars and moon were covered with clouds coming in from the north-east. It was then necessary for them to walk only for the benefit of each other. We are walking under the vigilance of no eyes at all, the doctor told himself, looking from her extraordinary face up to the dark and empty sky.

By a miracle, or through the strength of this rum love of theirs, they covered the four miles and reached the park which is no-man's-land in this present undeclared war. At night it is avoided by everyone except the junkies and jackals from both camps: but that night the wind was too cold even for them.

They were only a quarter of a mile into it when the doctor saw the irony of things. Not even the taxi-drivers came into the park at nights, because they were afraid, so nobody would find them until morning. And even under one of the scrubby bushes they would not stand a chance of survival through the night. Not at this temperature. Silence was already very shaky, with her eyes tightly closed; she was swaying on the point of collapse. The doctor no longer considered his own state of health. He talked to her, but even talking was pain in that wind. And as the clouds came over thicker it grew very very dark. Nobody could frighten them now.

Twice she collapsed. The second time he had to kick and swear at her and call her coward. He said terrible things to her, made obscene threats, then tugged and pulled until she was on her feet again. The park was as wide as a desert, it seemed, as cold as the Pole.

Then the doctor began to hear banging noises. He headed them towards the sounds until they heard machinery running and he knew they were near the railway. A long building loomed in front of them and as they got closer they were met by an undeniable odour and the desolate, restless lowing and kicking of cattle. The doctor thought of hoboes and thought of them, the two of them, riding the freight train with all the cattle. But then he remembered the cattle weren't going any further than this either.

They got in out of the wind and Silence collapsed and lay on her side in the straw. Engines juddered in the marshalling yards and shunted trucks clanged in unmelodic scales. The smell of disinfectant did battle with the animal smell and neither was winning. A door flapped on its hinges, trying to destroy itself in the wind. The doctor went off in search of it, the cattle didn't frighten him in the least, he felt he loved them. He felt he wanted to open all the doors and let them out into the park. He wanted to laugh. The wind tears were laughter tears starting before the laugh. Then there was a blood-curdling scream. For a second he thought it to be one of the animals. But when it came again he knew it was Silence's scream. He dashed back along the cattle pens.

Nothing terrible had happened. The big door had slammed shut at the other end and she'd woken up in the pitch dark. She must have thought she was in hell. He talked through her awful shouting and found her wrist and face and throat and told her funny silly truths and lies about how they were safe. 'For heaven's sake,' he said, 'we're in the best place. Give me animals any day. If we judge from the people we know. The cattle are lowing, a crib for a bed.' Again it was the tone, not the words. She steadied and he managed to coax her into the warmth of the house itself. The doctor arranged some clean straw as best he could, and she sank back in it. She lay on her tummy half beside and half across him with her head in his neck. Almost at once and together, they slept.

* * *

At 7 a.m. they began to move the cattle to the slaughterhouses. By 8 a.m. the doctor had betrayed her.

A slaughterhouse is very like a hospital. At an unearthly hour the doors were slid back and the lights switched on. The slaughtermen and porters came in noisily, shouting to each other and waking the dozy cattle. Silence was still alive and still asleep trustingly in his arms. He simply thought, I'm damned if I'll wake her to pain. Moreover, he wasn't feeling like exercise himself. Half cramped by the weight of her body, but also weakened by his wound and the exertions of escape he felt almost incapable of movement.

Of course, it wasn't long until someone spotted them. In fact it was a uniformed porter who seemed at that time of the morning to find it hard to believe his eyes. He was at first startled, then amused because he thought they were junkies or lovers. Then he looked defensive and concerned. He called to his buddy who was already wheeling great carcasses of meat through from the other side. The doctor thought, This is a place where delicacy is not observed. There was a great deal of noise by now in this echoing place and the cattle waited patiently.

Two more came over and a fat one who had been at work with a shovel and sounded Irish recognized the two of them.

'That's her,' he said at a glance, 'that's the one they call Silence. That's the one they want.'

Then looking at the doctor he snapped his fingers. 'Jesus!'

'Ewing,' the doctor said.

'That's it,' he said.

Their subsequent actions were enough to kill any kind feelings the doctor might still have entertained for the citizens of this city. The fat porter knew he was on to something of value. Even in his profession he must have seen something of the state of the pair, but he could have had no finer feelings, no compassion. None. 'You two stay exactly where you are. Just you two stay there. D'you hear me? You stay absolutely still.' He sounded threatening.

The cattle bellowed, frightened, smelling hot blood. The young man had a hurried conference with the other after which he called out, 'Down the middle, fifty-fifty,' as he hurried away stumbling. Silence still slept.

A moment later the doors at both ends were shut. Their bolts clanged home. In another couple of minutes the uniformed one and the fat Irishman appeared back. He had a little camera. It had a flash-bulb, and that woke up Silence.

Something about her yellow eyes, or the sudden

movement of her head, must have surprised or even alarmed the onlookers—and now there were ten or twelve of them—at the other side of the iron bars. In embarrassed reaction there was a little titter of laughter.

The doctor said, 'Close your eyes.'

A moment later some big policemen shouldered their way through. There was one quite senior man. He was extremely nice and polite. He said, 'Thank God you're alive, doctor,' and told his assistant to clear everybody else out. The porter had taken another two snapshots. He had what he needed.

Then the inner door was unlocked and two officers crawled through. The doctor told them to be very careful of Silence. They said, 'Don't you worry, doc, we will be,' and for a second the doctor could not or would not understand the way they said that. They helped her through the door of the pen civilly enough while the doctor explained about her hands and her back. They assimilated the information without any show of emotion. They're trained that way, the doctor thought.

The one thing the doctor had told her was that he would not leave her. The manner of his betrayal was spectacular. By the time he emerged into the open where two or three police cars were now gathered, he knew there was danger. He was thinking, You have to see both sides to recognize how hostile your own side can look. They were implacable. They had already handcuffed her and somebody had cautioned her. As soon as the doctor came out they helped him. Two men even shook his hand. They seemed to think that he had brought Silence back to Justice. Why not? She had murdered his son.

The doctor's head felt very sore in the cold wind. He asked that he could go in the same car with Silence. They just said, 'No, no.' He tried to insist for a moment and again they reassured him that she'd be treated fine. 'Wrapped in cotton wool,' one said. 'Don't … ' the doctor began. And he'd wanted to say, Don't make her talk.

When he looked across at Silence, who was about to be put in one of the cars, she did not seem upset. There was no yell, no terrible plea in her eyes. She seemed to expect the separation and to be resigned, quite resigned to it.

The doctor spread out his arms, looked down at his wound, saw the mess, the bloody, pussy mess, and felt his knees begin to collapse.

'Catch him,' an officer yelled. But too late. He was out, in the snow.

* * *

About a week later, all the newspapers had it that Ewing was recovering well, after three very dangerous days. His mother had been to visit him but had only stayed a few moments. The doctor still seemed too painful to speak. The police had no further information about the girl called 'Silence': she was being held.

'Is it true,' one journalist asked, 'that she can't speak?'

'I don't know about that,' the spokesman replied. 'But she'll talk.'

The report of that reply was what made the doctor determined to get up. The police doctors had been very good to him. In fact both he and Silence were in the same wing though neither knew it. She was only two floors above, in a more heavily guarded section. The hospital itself was fundamentally for policemen and attached to the Central Police Station.

They allowed him up and gave him back his clothes. He had, be it remembered, been involved in a fight which led to the death of a twelve-year-old coloured boy. When they returned his clothes to him now, he found that they hadn't even searched them. In his breast pocket he could still feel the dentist's slim, steel surgical knife.

Before formal questioning, they wanted him to have a few hours' relaxation. The officers in charge of him (who couldn't have been more warm and friendly to him) gave each other a wink and said they might take a little time off between the Hospital and the Station.

The doctor did not see the force of the joke until he was taken across the street into a bar which he soon discovered was also just outside the Station. It was strictly a policemen's bar with a few good looking policemen's molls — keep your hands off that one, fella, that's the sergeant's girl.

Here again the doctor found himself to be something of a hero. The barman wanted to shake him by the hand. Only one of the girls seemed to think that he had brought Silence back for some other reason than vengeance. She'd seen the stockyard photo. 'She really seemed to be trusting you.'

Answer: 'Yes, she did.'

Because something had been said that might spoil the party, the boys poured out more drinks. The doctor was a difficult guest of honour. They took him aside to tell him to stop worrying. Through this creature Silence they were going to get every man and woman that touched Junior. Every bastard in that lynching. And they said it again, 'Don't you worry, we'll make her talk.' When they said that the ice in the doctor's whisky began to tinkle against the glass.

He played along with them as best he could, because he wanted a favour. There were several charges against her. She already had this police record. They told him that. She was conscious. She was being looked after mainly by women, but with a coloured doctor. 'Now you can't be fairer than that.' Eventually they divulged that she was in the same building.

The doctor asked to see her as soon as they were back in the building. The policemen couldn't understand why. The doctor didn't want to explain except to say that together they had been through some tough experiences. The policemen seemed to appreciate that. They thought of it, perhaps, as a man who wanted to look at his retrograde dog. They detailed an officer to go up with him. Someone said that they'd been looking for him all over, that Lilian and Angel had come to visit him. Lilian was fine, fine.

He was introduced to the young coloured surgeon on the wing who was not too impressive, the doctor thought. Police-trained. The strange thing is that the doctor telegraphed the whole thing to him, but he was far too dumb to see it. The doctor said—about nothing—'It's bad when they cut the jugular, doctor.' The younger man did not look at the doctor as if he thought he was cracked; he said, 'It's also pretty quick.'

'What's pretty, doctor?'

'It isn't too pretty, I guess.'

He must have thought the doctor was referring to Lawrence Junior or one of the others.

'But they wouldn't sense too much. There's some kind of misting up,' the doctor added. The doctor had been prepared to sit outside the ward in which the girl was kept, but another policeman on guard there unbolted the door, saying, 'She's pretty sleepy, don't think you'll get much sense.'

The doctor went into the little blazingly white room. The door wasn't locked behind him, but pushed almost closed. The knife was in his pocket still.

He asked her. Of course he asked her. The second he went into the room, he said, 'They're going to make you talk.'

And she shook her head. He let his eyes fall from hers to the column, the strong column of her neck. She turned painfully on to her side. She always liked it if he pushed her head against him. He pressed it against his own wound so it hurt very badly. The voice behind him said, 'Please don't do that.'

But he dropped his head on to her sweet, strong

still surviving heart and thanked God. Thanked God that dentists keep sweet, sharp knives.

Then there was blood over everybody and a hell of a lot of people seemed to be there. He stood. He kept his eyes on her until he knew suddenly and gloriously that she was dead. He wiped the tears from his face with his sleeve, then he spoke. He said levelly, 'Notice the blood. It is also red.'

He now seemed to be beyond sadness. Then he turned and looked at all the others who were still standing round in an appalling silence. He said, 'Now, please will somebody take me away?'

There followed a bloody accusing confusion and crying noise.